DUSTY'S FAMILY

Don Dewey

Copyright 2023

ISBN: 9798398109580

WWII

10,000 miles apart.

Fell in love through letters.

Met in person three years later.

A wild Australian dog saved the life of the young soldier.

Dusty became the protector of the young woman from a small coal mining town in Kentucky when they met.

A love story—a war story

In the center was a loyal dog.

Contents

Dusty's Family 1
Dusty's Family 5
Joe 9
Dusty 54
Hazel 56
Dusty and Joe 80
10,000 Mile Courtship 106
End of the War 124
The Wedding 182
The Big Move 191
New Life 195
Dusty's Family 201
More Pictures 206
Group Discussion Guide 214
Books by Don Dewey 216

DUSTY'S FAMILY

I hid in the grass. I was small enough to be shorter than the grass when I flattened on my belly.

The men came and my dad tried to defend us. He fought them and hurt two. Then they shot him. Mom jumped in to help, but they shot her too. Then they started searching the brush—for me I guess. I had no idea why my parents were killed, but it left me an orphan—alone and too small to survive on my own. Still, I hid, and finally they went away.

I poked at my parents, once at a time, then I pulled at them, but they wouldn't move. I'd seen enough dead animals to know they were dead. I snuggled up to my mom, feeling the warmth of her body. That was better, but something was still wrong. Oh, I couldn't feel the beat of her heart.

In the early morning when I woke up, mom was cold. Both of them were stiff in death. I yelled to the sky in my grief, and then headed out, knowing I'd die soon too.

My immediate need was water. I was so thirsty. Making my way to water was the scariest part of every day. That day, without my parents, was the worst ever. There were things all over that place that would eat anybody they could catch. But I was so thirsty I had to try it on my own. I lowered my head and lapped up some water. I hadn't had anything to drink in two days, so I needed a lot. As I drank, a fat, furry critter came to the water's edge a few feet away. I didn't know him or anything about his kind, but we were both there to drink, so we ignored each other. Then a huge thing with a mouth bigger than me shot out of the water and grabbed him by his head and shoulders. His furry body struggled, but he got dragged into the water by the long-mouthed creature. I learned later people called it a crocodile. I was very careful at the watering hole after that.

The next year I lived alone. I killed small animals and the occasional fat rabbit to live, and more than anything else I wanted a family again. I survived and that surprised me. I *grew bigger, although I stayed pretty skinny. There was never enough to eat.*

My life got interesting when I met my best friend and his buddies. A long time later he found a female and our family got bigger. Then little humans came along, and I had my work cut out for me, 'cause I helped take care of them. That's okay because my pack is complete now.

Did I mention that I'm a wild dog, born and raised in Australia? That's where I met Joe. I almost died when my parents were killed, and I almost died when I saved Joe's life. My friend, Joe, thinks I'm part Dingo, 'cause of my pointy ears, and part, well, some other kind of dog. Who knows? I don't really care, so long as I have my friend. Meeting him was the best day ever.

These are my pack – I shared my life with them, and they with me. Now we're sharing it with you.

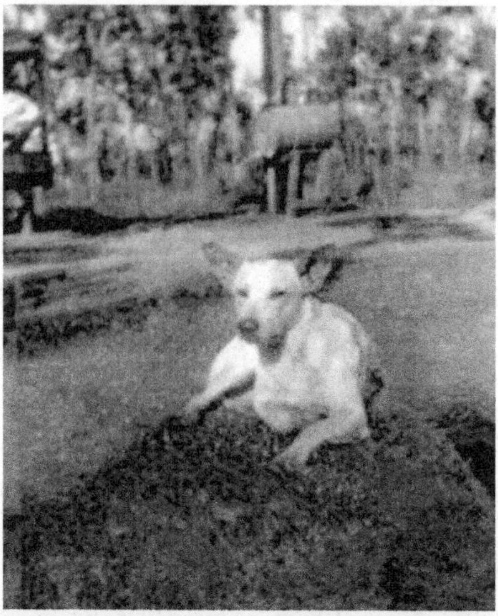

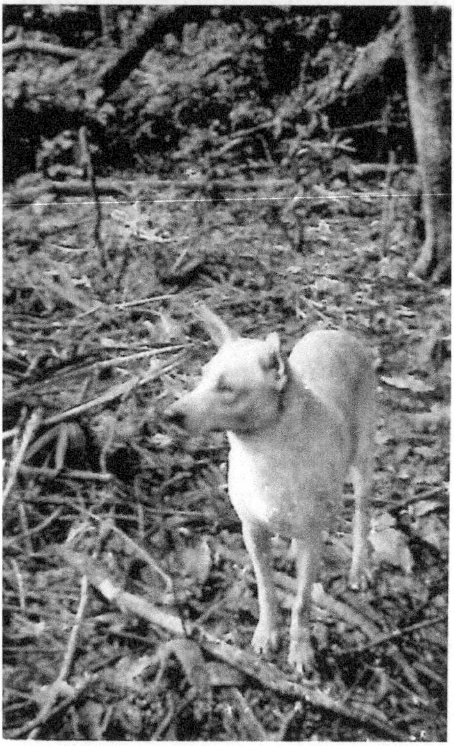

JOE

Stuart Dewey had his three children lined up in front of him. "Children, your mother has died. Remember I told you this was going to happen soon. Serena, go to your room. I'll talk with you later. Florence, you and Wilbur come with me." He took his young son's hand while his slightly older daughter followed them into the bedroom. They walked slowly past the large-flowered wallpaper in the hall, then into the bedroom with its lavender paper, speckled with tiny flowers. The man and the boy stood quietly by the bed while little Florence knelt by the bed and began to cry. She rubbed her mother's arm, then ran out of the room sobbing. Wilbur looked up at his father. "How come Serena's not here?"

"Your little sister is too young for this. I'll speak with her later. You heard me send her to her room."

The window shades were pulled down and the lamp next to the four postered bed was on, its dim bulb barely lighting the room through the dark shade. As Wilbur stood by his parents' bed he reached out his little hand for his mother and touched her. "She feels kind of cool."

"I know, Son. Her body will lose all its warmth now that she's gone."

"Gone? But she's right here. Won't she wake up?"

"No, Son. I told you—your mother died. Her soul went to heaven, and we'll bury her body in a couple of days."

Small, teary eyes turned to look up at Stuart Dewey. "Out back, like we buried the cat?" Tears started rolling down the puffy cheeks.

"No—well, kind of. You'll see in a couple of days. There's a special place we call a cemetery. It's like a big park with lots of grass and flowers, and that's where we bury people when they die. All our relatives and friends will come to the funeral. Some of our relatives you never knew are buried there."

Wilbur hung on the side of the bed, refusing to let go of his mother's hand. Finally his father pulled him roughly away from his deceased mother and sent him to bed. Stuart Dewey sat in the near dark alone, silently, as he waited for the undertaker to come.

He didn't notice his son watching him from the stairs.

*** * ****

His father was a stern man who soon took another wife twenty years his junior. With three young children and the farm he needed help.

Florence seemed to move through everything calmly, while his youngest girl. Serena, was emotional about most things. Wilbur was measured and thoughtful, yet things seemed to pile up on him to give him a troubled childhood. He was a loner, a scrapper and never felt like he fit in. He didn't know what to make of this new development.

"You're not my mother, Mildred." His little face was screwed up in a grimace.

"Of course not, Wilbur, but I'm going to take good care of you, your sisters and your father."

"I don't need no takin' care of. I'm just fine, thank you."

Mildred didn't smile much. She just stared at this tiny first grader for a minute. "I don't think you should call me 'Mildred.' If you don't want to call me, 'mom,' let's think of something else."

"How about, 'mam?'"

She sighed. "I'm sorry, Wilbur, that I've not been around children much, but if you want to call me, 'ma'am,' that's quite alright."

"My name isn't Wilbur. It's Joe."

"That's your middle name, isn't it?"

"So what? I'm Joe."

"If your father says that's okay, then it's alright with me. You had best speak with him about it. You know he feels quite sternly about a lot of things, and I've never heard him mention his son, Joe. Just Wilbur. Go on now."

He hated his name and went straight to his father to tell him about his decision to go by his middle name, Joe. His father completely dismissed the notion. "Wilbur is your name. Your middle name is not what you're going to be known by. You're going to be Wilbur. Your name has always been Wilbur, and it is still Wilbur. Besides, your sisters both go by their first names. You can too."

Little Joe held his ground and faced off with his father. "I am Joe. I am *not* Wilbur."

Stuart knelt down to his son's height. He looked him in the eyes and spoke very slowly and with great emphasis. "Your – name – is – Wilbur. That's enough of this nonsense."

Despite Stuart's attempt to shut it down, the argument went on for weeks. Stuart finally had enough and didn't want to fight his little boy any longer. "You can use any of your names you want; just pick one. Son, say, I can call you that, can't I? Son, I'm just tired of arguing about this, so go by whatever you want. I guess it really doesn't matter much. Whatever you choose, stay with it. You can't keep changing your mind.

"I noticed you call Mildred, 'ma'am.' You should probably call her, 'mom.'"

"She's not my mom. I was gonna call her 'Mildred,' but she said I pro'ly shouldn't call her by her given name, so I'm going to call her, 'mam.'"

His father just sighed. He'd learned how stubborn his son was, and just wasn't willing to argue with him about these things anymore. "Go on, Son. Get ready for dinner. 'Ma'am' will have it ready soon."

His son just looked at him funny, wondering if his dad was making fun of him. With rare wisdom for his tender age, he decided to ignore it.

* * *

Even in grade school people seemed mean to Wilbur, now going by Joe. People saw things in him they said were handicaps—that made him feel like he was crippled in some way.

His teacher, Ms. Fawcett, had several problems with Joe. The first one was his name. "But your name is Wilbur. It says so on your registration form. You see, it's right there." She held the paper out to Joe and pointed to his name.

Joe leaned into the paper and looked at it carefully. He couldn't read much yet, but he had learned some. He certainly knew how to spell his name—all three of them.

He pointed to the name also. "Yes Ms. Fawcett, but it also says, 'Joseph,' right there. I have three names—they're right there. Sometimes my dad calls me by all three, usually when he's mad at me about something. Here at school I'm not Wilbur, I'm not Joey, and I'm not Joseph—I'm just, 'Joe.'"

Ms. Fawcett made a noise in her throat. "Humph."

This became a running argument, but unlike his father, his teacher wasn't going to put up with it. She ignored his wishes and called him, Wilbur.

His teacher also had a real issue with how he wrote. Joe took his paper and turned it around 180°. Then he twisted his left arm around and wrote with the top of the letters pointing to him. The children were just learning to write and were focused on basic penmanship with simple words. "Wilbur, why do you insist on twisting the paper upside down to write? You have beautiful penmanship; look at the lovely loop you put in the 'g' in 'dog'. But you need to learn to use your right hand—that's normal. People just don't write with their left hands."

"I do, Ma'am."

"Well, don't."

"I have to. I can't make the letters with my right hand. You said I write okay."

"Yes, but you don't go about it properly. Use your other hand. Just do it." She smacked his desk with her ruler for emphasis.

He glared at her in defiance and tried his right hand. *I'd like to smack her with that stupid ruler she carries around. On the outside I'm being polite lady, but on the inside I'm sticking my tongue out and calling you names.*

She smiled at him then, which just made her look meaner to him, then walked away to monitor the rest of the class. He watched her walk away, turned the paper so the top was facing his chest, pulled it close, and wrote with his left hand.

In his teacher's expert opinion, his rebellious habits had to end. She pondered whether to make the issue his name or his refusal to write with the proper hand. She chose to start with his name. She wrote a carefully worded note to Wilbur's father to gain his support. That night Joe had to give his father the note from Ms. Fawcett. They sat together while Stuart read it aloud.

Mr. Dewey,

Wilbur has determined to not respond to his name. He only answers to 'Joe.'" I believe this to be highly unusual and would like him to accept his given name in class. Certainly it is your decision. Please advise me how to proceed.
Sincerely,
Ms. Fawcett, First Grade Teacher.

Stuart looked at Joe. He smiled slightly. "I told you this would be a problem. What do you think I should do?"

"I think you should tell her my name is Joe. I'm not gonna let her call me Wilbur. I told her at school I wasn't Wilbur, Joey or Joseph. I'm Joe."

"Would you like to write the note?"

Joe looked at his feet, "No sir. I can't spell all the words I would need."

So be it. I'll pen a note tonight, and you can take it to her tomorrow. Would you like to hear it? I can write it now and read it to you as I do."

"Yes sir."

"Very well. I'll compose it now." He wrote slowly, speaking each word aloud.

Dear Ms. Fawcett,

Thank you for asking for clarification on this matter. I'm sure you have found my son to be inordinately determined. The issue with his name has been settled to my satisfaction. He goes by his middle name, which is of course, 'Joe.' Thank you for accepting this unorthodox nomenclature.
Sincerely,
Stuart Dewey

He looked at his silent son. "Well, what do you think?"

"What's 'nomenclater' mean?"

"Nomenclature. It simply means the words you choose to label or describe something, and you have chosen Joe."

"Perfect. Thank you, sir. I don't want to be called two different names at different places. This will work out swell."

"Very well. I'll fold this and put it in your lunch box. Take it with your lunch tomorrow and give it to your teacher."

Joe hopped up with a big grin on his tiny face and headed outside to see if there were any bunnies grazing on the clover near their fields. He loved to throw things at them and watch them run.

* * *

Joe moved up to second grade with his class and left Ms. Fawcett behind. His new teacher was Mrs. Twitchell. The school was rural, and as such it was a racially mixed grade school; at least some classrooms were integrated. There weren't enough of any minority race to rate a separate school building.

A few months into second grade Mrs. Twitchell gave the class what she believed was a fun and creative assignment. Every day included some coloring time, but today's assignment would tell her a bit of what they thought their world looked like. She was quite impressed with her idea of having them color things they saw, together, as a group every day. Mrs. Twitchell addressed the class with her rehearsed voice, which she believed was warm and friendly. "Children, you each have a picture of a classroom, much like our own. Color in the picture, including the children in it. Make everything as accurate as you can. Make it look like real life, and we'll display the pictures in the hall so everyone can enjoy them."

Young Joe looked at the crayons and read the colors on them, then looked around at the classroom. He stared at different kids, trying to assess the proper color for each one. He decided on a color for one of the boys in the picture, and another color for the other children in it. He worked hard on coloring it in, then showed it to his teacher. He was beaming with pride on the fine job he thought he'd done.

"What were you thinking Joe? No one is that color." She pointed to the child he colored green in the picture. "That's a ridiculous picture. Start over and do it right." She tore his picture in half rather dramatically.

Joe didn't get teary, he got mad. He stood to his full four-foot height, stared at his teacher, and pointed at an

African American boy in his class. "The crayon says 'green' on it. Lamont's as green as that crayon."

"He is not—don't you try to say he is."

"He is!" Joe held his ground. "It's true and you know it. Why aren't you telling the truth? You're the teacher—you're supposed to tell us the truth!"

"Go back to your seat, Joe. Be quiet and I'll talk with you later."

Joe went back to his seat with his torn picture. The other children were cruel, as children often are.

"That's stupid, Joe."

"You can't even color right."

"Green kids. What a dope."

"What a retard."

The kids near his seat taunted him until one boy jumped up and stuck his face close to Joe. "What color am I, Dummy?"

Joe didn't hesitate. He lurched forward from his chair and punched the boy, then fell back down hard in his seat. The boy screamed, held his nose with a trickle of blood running through his fingers, and just stood there wailing.

Ms. Twitchell was a big woman, but she reacted quickly. "Who hit you, Johnny?"

Through his bloody fingers Johnny whimpered, "Joe did."

"Joe, I'm going to have to speak to your parents about this. You can't lie and fight like this in class." He glared at her the rest of the day. *I know she's wrong, and I know she's lying, but I can't figure out why.*

That night, with his lower lip trembling, he sat in the living room prepared to face his father. Since his mother died when he was small and his father's new wife, Mildred, was a stern woman, he decided it was best to have it out with his dad. While his father was a hard man, he was also fair.

"Sit." Joe sat and looked at his shoes. "Your teacher says you lied in class Joe, and then you beat up another boy. Is that true?"

"No, it's not."

"Your teacher sent me the picture you colored. I see it's torn in half. Did you do that?

"No sir. The teacher did, in front of everybody. She said the way I colored it was stupid."

"It certainly looks like you colored a little boy green. You know that's not right."

"It *is* right. Three kids in my class are that color."

Stuart turned to his desk and lifted the two pieces of Joe's picture. "This boy you colored surely looks green to me, and I've never seen a green person."

"Well, I have. Three of them are in my class, and more than that are in my school."

Stuart was silent for a full minute as he looked from the picture to his son and back again. "Bring me the crayons you have here at home. Run and get them. Let's figure this out."

"Yes sir." Joe hustled to his room to get his crayon box. He solemnly handed it to his father, each thin, waxy stick of color standing stiffly upright in its place, nestled close to the others. All the pointy ends were facing up, and most of the paper sleeves were intact. It was very tidy.

His dad lifted out one crayon and held it out. Joe couldn't see the name of the color from his angle, but his father could. It said, 'black.' Stuart let Joe look at the crayon for a moment in silence. "Is the boy in your class this color?"

"Yes sir."

Stuart held out another crayon for his son to look at. Again, he hid the name, which was 'green.' "Or was he this color?"

"That's the same color. So yeah, he's that color."

"How many crayons in the box are the color of the green boy? Take your time and look at them all, then tell me how many are the same."

Joe looked at them very seriously, studying the crayons before he answered. "It's hard to say, sir, but eight, I think. Eight are the same color, but some are lighter than others. I've wondered my whole life why they put so many of the same ones in the box but give them different names."

Stuart chuckled. "Your whole life, huh? Well, I suppose it has been a lifetime for you. Sit right there Joe, while I collect some things for us to use." Joe watched patiently as his father walked around the room, then disappeared into the kitchen, picking up various little things. He set out several pieces of paper with differing colors on them. Some were from magazines and others were scraps that he found around the house. There were even pieces of fabric of various colors.

"Which ones are the same color? Just stack them up together. All the ones that are the same color, even if they're lighter or darker."

Joe did. He put green, black, purple and several other colors together and said they were the same. He put white, yellow and beige in another pile.

His dad sighed. "Well, that's the problem. You're colorblind. You don't see all the colors other people see. You'll have to learn how to do things in black and white and gray. You know, I believe I read that dogs are colorblind too, and see things only in black, white and gray. That's how you see, too—like a dog. I'm sorry Son, but this isn't going away—ever. It's a tough break, but you created part of your own problems. You won't go by your first name, which your teachers want you to use, you're left-handed and you refuse to learn how to write with your right hand, which will be a problem your entire life, and now we find that you're colorblind. Very unfortunate. Well, you'll learn how to manage it with time.

"Now, about the fighting. Did you punch Johnny in the face?"

"Yes sir."

"Why?"

"A bunch of kids made fun of me after the teacher tore up my picture, and Johnny put his face right up to me and called me a dummy. So I hit him."

"So, the boy, this Johnny, provoked you."

"Yes sir, he pervoked me, and I fixed him."

Stuart looked at his son for a long time before he replied. He finally sighed again. "Well, okay then. It's after your bedtime already, so off to bed with you."

A tearful little boy went to bed that night, and it was the beginning of some tough years for him.

* * *

Life didn't get any easier for Joe. At nine years of age he ran away from home for the first time. Stuart and Mildred called everyone they could think of, but there was no sign of Joe.

Joe was kicking back in a hayloft enjoying a fresh apple he'd just picked. The barn door opened—he dove for cover, but the hay in the loft was loose and it started a slide that landed him on some bales down below. The hay kept sliding down and piling up for the longest time. Joe was buried in it. He shook the hay off and stood up. "Just what are you doing in my barn, and who are you?" The old farmer squinted at him. "You're Stuart Dewey's boy, aren't you?"

"I'm sorry sir. I didn't mean to cause any trouble. I was just taking a nap and you startled me."

"My question was, 'What are you doing here?'"

The farmer had been inching closer as they spoke. Joe started to answer him and the old guy moved faster than Joe expected, and had him by the arm.

Three days after Joe disappeared the Dewey's phone rang. "Hello?"

"Stuart? This is Marve Saunders up the road. I got something of yours."

"What's that, Marve?"

"What'er you missin'?"

"You found Joe?"

"Got a grip on him right now. Found him in my barn. Don't know why, don't care to know. Can you come get him?"

So ended Joe's first runaway trip. His second came a year later, and he got all the way to Detroit. The police brought him back that time.

They say the third time's the charm. He left again and stayed away for six months. He was fifteen years old and hitched rides north until he got to a Civilian Conservation Corps (CCC) Camp. They were almost military. They gave young men clothing, food, and the men worked on projects for the good of the country. From 1933 to 1942 the organization employed young men from eighteen to twenty-five years of age.

"Son, this program is for men eighteen or older. You don't look it."

"Just turned eighteen sir. That's why I'm here."

"I guess if you can pass the fingerprint test, and we don't find drugs in you, you can try to pass the physical exam. How's that sound?"

"Sounds good. How much does it pay?"

"Right to the point, huh? Thirty dollars a month. You live here and we give you three squares a day. We can send twenty-five dollars of that home to your family if you like."

"No thanks. I'll take it."

I've never been fingerprinted, so that's good, and I've never used any drugs, so that's okay. The physical part of this will be a cinch.

Three months later he was dropped from the program—they found out he was too young. He never knew how they figured it out.

Joe was seventeen when he left home for the last time. Florence had already married and Serena was still a kid. *I'm not going to run away—I've done that too many times. I'm psyched and ready to tell them I'm going, and I expect they'll be glad to let me go without an argument. I guess they could argue it, but I'm leaving one way or another.*

He told them as they were seated at dinner. "Dad, Mildred, I have to tell you something."

Stuart's head came up sharply and he opened his mouth to respond to his son calling his stepmother by her given name, but Mildred put her hand on his and squeezed. Her look told him to let it go. Uncharacteristically, he did. "What do you need to tell us, Joe?"

"I'm going to Tennessee. I'm going to work at the Tennessee Valley Authority."

Serena rolled her eyes. "Again?"

"Not again. This is different. And it's none of your business, Sis."

Stuart spoke firmly to his daughter. "Go to your room Serena. Take your plate and eat there. We have to discuss some things."

"But Daddy..."

"Go!"

Serena picked up her plate with an exaggerated sigh and headed for the stairs.

"Why Joe? You can stay here and work on the farm. I thought that's what we decided."

"With all due respect, sir, that's what *you* decided. I don't want to work on the farm. I'm leaving on Monday."

"How will you go?"

"I'll take the bus. I saved bus fare and I can make enough money there to pay for what I need."

Stuart sat quietly and simply stared at his son for a long moment. *I'm not going to argue with this headstrong boy. It's never been very effective.* "If that's what you want, then I guess it's okay with me. Mildred and I will see you off on Monday. We'll drive you to the bus station. I have to tell you, Son, that you have been one difficult child. All the trouble at school, running away time after time, and now this!"

Joe spoke in a quiet, calm voice. "Well, you didn't have to tell me that, Dad. Obviously, I already knew it. And you saying it doesn't give me any more reasons to stay home. I'm sorry for the trouble I've been, but you know, I didn't choose to be left-handed, or colorblind, or to have mom die. Sorry Mildred, you've been great. All that's just part of my life, and now I want to figure out what to do with the rest of my life. I don't think I can do that here."

Joe stood up straight, pushed back his chair and walked out of the room. Stuart and Mildred finished their meal in silence.

Monday came—Stuart and Mildred took their boy and their teenaged daughter to the bus station. Stuart pulled his car into a space and turned off the ignition. "You sure about this?"

"Yes Sir."

The four of them walked together to the window and Joe bought his ticket. Stuart excused himself and left for the restroom while Mildred, Joe and Serena sat to wait.

Mildred handed Joe some bills, neatly folded. "It isn't much, but it will help you eat, at least, when you get there. I'll miss you."

Joe took the money with obvious hesitation. "Does Dad know you're giving me this?"

"No, and it doesn't matter. It's my money."

"You know I respect you, and I will always love you for doing what my mom couldn't be there to do."

"I know that."

"Your name is Mildred, so that's probably what I'll always call you, no matter what Dad thinks."

"That's okay with me. I'll speak to your father and tell him that's what I want you to call me."

Stuart returned and gave his son a brief hug. "Come, Mildred. Let's go."

She stood and gave Joe an uncharacteristically long, hearty hug. "Be good." For the first time since Mildred had come into his life, Joe saw tears in her eyes.

Little Serena jumped in and gave her big brother a hug and clung to him, quietly crying. "I'll miss you Joe."

"I'll miss you too, squirt. But I'll write, and I'll visit. You're gonna marry and have some great kids and a good life. I know it."

She let go of him and fled for the car.

Stuart and Mildred left him standing there, feeling a bit unsure about this new adventure.

* * *

His first bus ride was from Michigan to Tennessee. He knew there was work there, and he wanted to be on his own. He walked for what seemed forever, then opened the door to a local Tennessee Valley Authority office.

This is it, I guess. I'm sure they'll believe me. "Hello sir, I'd like to apply for a job."

"Not sure you're old enough, son."

"I'm not your son, and I'm plenty old enough. How old do you have to be to work for the Tennessee Valley Authority? I thought FDR wanted to give everyone a chance to work."

"Well, that's true, son. Sorry—young man. How old are you anyway?"

"Eighteen. Is that old enough?"

"Just. You're sure about that age, right? You wouldn't be kidding me?"

"Of course I am. I know how old I am. You know how old you are, don't you?"

"Alright, don't get your panties in a twist, kid. You're all set. Come back in the morning at 7:00 and we'll put you on the job. If you're late, you can take your eighteen-year-old butt somewhere else to look for a job."

"Yes sir. I'll be here." With a big grin the seventeen-year-old boy walked out, ready to be a man the next day. However, with almost no money, the clothes he was wearing, and a small bag with clothes, a toothbrush and small items, it would be a long night. He pulled out his wallet and counted his bills again. *Man, three nights in a cheap hotel will break me. Thanks, Mildred, but it wasn't enough.*

He stopped walking when he saw other guys close to his age sleeping in a park. *At least it's a lot warmer than Michigan. This will work out just fine.* "You guys gonna work for the TVA too?"

A lanky, strawberry blond kid looked him up and down. Then he grinned. "Sure. I've been there for two weeks. Tommy just started two days ago, and the guys on those benches I don't know."

Tommy rolled off his bench and stuck out his hand. They shook. "What's your name?"

"Joe Dewey. Just got here today, and I start work tomorrow."

"You eighteen? You don't look eighteen. But Jerry don't either really, but he swears he is, and I'm nineteen, really, honest I am."

"Take a breath, Tommy. Nobody cares how old we are. We got jobs, they'll sell us hootch, and we'll get a real place to stay soon. It's about money, not how old we are."

Tommy stuck his chin out at Jerry, kind of pointing. "Jerry seems older than any of us, but he sure don't look it."

"Nice to meet you guys. I guess I'll take this bench over here."

"Help yourself. They're first come, first served."

They all settled in as best they could. The night was cool but not cold, and the streetlight was far enough away that it was dark enough to sleep. Joe was more tired than nervous, so he dropped off quickly. His last thought as he drifted off was, *If Dad saw me sleeping on a park bench he'd call me a bum.*

Joe woke up with his right ankle hurting. He was in the park, and it took a few seconds for him to remember that. A guy was trying to pull his shoes off him without untying them, and it hurt. He kicked at the man. "Stop it! What the hell you doin'?"

The man stood up and kicked Joe. "Shut up, kid, and give me your shoes."

"They're mine." He stood up and faced his attacker. Joe wasn't his grown height yet, but he was a muscular five-feet-six inches. The stranger sucker punched him in the stomach, then swung his right fist at him hard. That was when Joe realized he could fight. He was quick. He dodged and swung back with his strong left fist. To his surprise the man's eyes rolled back, he toppled backwards and just lay there. Several park residents were awake now and gathered round, asking questions while Joe shook his hand like it was on fire. "This jerk tried to steal my shoes. They're mine!"

"Damn buddy, that's Mitch, and he's tough. He takes whatever he wants. You know, he's one of the reasons we don't have enough money yet for a place to stay. Did you kill him?"

Jerry was staring at the man on the ground. "He sure looks dead." He poked him with his toe.

"All I did was hit him. I think I broke a finger. Jerk. He kicked me first. Nobody's taking my stuff. I got too little already."

"You know, you could make some money as a fighter. Golden Gloves or something. Ever thought about it?"

"Never even heard of it."

"Don't matter anyway I guess. Tommy here said the Germans may start another war pretty soon, so none of this is gonna matter to us."

"What will you guys do? I mean, if a war does start."

"Sign up, I guess. Guys?" Jerry looked around at the young men bunched up in the dim light of a streetlamp.

They either agreed or didn't know what they thought. Nobody disagreed with fighting for their country.

Joe was thoughtful. "I'm not old enough to sign up."

Tommy spoke up. "So what? I bet you weren't old enough to get a job here either."

"Well, yeah. But that's different."

"Why?"

"I don't know. It just is."

Jerry jumped in. "I'm seventeen today and my birthday's six months away. But if the USA gets into a war next week, all of a sudden I'm eighteen and they'll take me. I guarantee it."

Jerry poked Joe's arm. "Hey fightin' man, what's your name, anyways?"

"Joe Dewey. I just got here today."

"Well, I'm serious about you fighting for money. You should check it out."

"I'll think about it. I sure don't want to go back home. My stepmom is okay, but she's not my mom. My dad's an old man and he drinks too much. I gotta be on my own."

* * *

A few weeks went by and Joe and the guys he hung out with were all making more money at the Tennessee Valley

Authority than they'd ever seen. They rented a room together, which was too crowded, but it was theirs. They went out drinking a fair amount and spent too much of their pay on it. What they didn't spend on booze they lost gambling. Poker was the game, and most of them weren't very good. Joe was about average and lost a bit more than he won.

A couple of them liked to sing, so when they were sauced they often sang along at a local nightclub. They got pretty good at lying about their age, but nobody checked too closely with all these young guys trying to get rid of their pay. Tonight they cleaned up and headed for what they thought of as, "their night club."

The line at the door was moving quickly. The bouncer was six and half feet tall with a deep ebony skin tone. He looked everyone over before he waved them on. "Whoa. I think I got to throw you boys back. You don't look the legal limit."

"C'mon, we come all the time. You know us. We're all old enough to be here."

The big bouncer laughed a deep, throaty laugh. "Sure you are. And my sister is FDR's wife. Hell, go on in, but don't cause any trouble."

They settled in and started drinking. Jimmy was singing loudly along with the crooner on the stage. "Jimmy, knock it off, man! You're as loud as the guy on the stage."

Jimmy turned to Tommy. "So what?" He kept on singing along.

Joe had too much to drink and started singing along with him. "I love this song, guys. I can sing this song."

"Hey man, maybe they'll hire you to sing up there and entertain everybody!"

Amidst laughter from his friends, he took up the challenge. "I *am* gonna sing it up there, like that guy!" Joe staggered to his feet. He went up on the stage, pushed the singer away and took his mic. The music wavered as the band began to stop, but Joe waved them on and started singing. The band was game, so they kept playing. His buddies started clapping and cheering, and then other people joined in. That was when Joe realized he could sing.

The two bouncers stood with the manager and watched Joe on the stage. "Hey, I kind of like that boy's singin', but after the song you guys do your job—toss him and his drunken friends out. I can't be havin' the audience take over." The bruisers both nodded. The song ended and they met Joe on his way back to his table. They escorted him the rest of the way.

"C'mon, guys. You got to leave now." There were four of them and two bouncers, but the bouncers were big. They each put one hand on two different guys, just so there was no misunderstanding.

All six were standing. Tommy shoved his bouncer. "I'm not done here yet."

"Oh yes you are." He tightened his grip and started moving Tommy and another guy toward the door.

Joe took offence. "Hey! He said he wasn't done yet. None of us are."

Joe's bouncer laughed and tried to move Joe and his other friend. Drunk as he was, Joe took a swing at the big guy. He connected pretty well, but the bouncer didn't drop like Mitch did in the park. He just got mad. "That's enough kid!" He let go of his second charge and grabbed Joe in a bearhug. He lifted him right off his feet and walked to the door. All the while Joe was yelling and struggling. The second bouncer herded the other three guys. They got to the door and Joe's buddies got frisky. One swung at the bouncer and another punched him in the gut. The bouncer was immovable. Jimmy shook his hand in the air. "Damn, that was like hittin' a wall." As he shook his aching hand, the bouncer twisted his arm behind his back and rammed him through the open door. Tommy came flying out after him and Jerry put his arms up to fend off the burley bouncer. "Out, kid! Now!"

Suddenly Tommy and Jimmy were bowled over by Jerry being hurled out. Joe's bouncer tossed him sideways after he stepped outside. All four guys lay on the sidewalk looking up. "Stay out for two weeks. Then you can come back. Any sooner and this will be worse." They stared mutely as the walking mountains moved back through the doorway.

They got up and dusted their clothes off. Jerry looked at the door. "Anybody want to go back inside?"

"Sure. I can take that ape!"

"Shut up Jimmy. You can't take him or you woulda done it."

There were no serious takers. Three of them just walked off. After a long moment of hesitation, Jimmy ran to catch up with his buddies.

They all showed up for work the next day bruised and hung over.

※ ※ ※

A few weeks later Joe started throwing more money around than his new buddies. "What's up with the cash, Dewey?"

"Yeah, and how come your hand's bandaged up? How'd you hurt it?"

"You guys talked me into boxing, remember? I didn't like not being able to handle those bruisers at the club either, so I signed up for Golden Gloves. I've been winning. You guys should come to a match now that I know my way around."

"Sure thing!" Joe's five buddies all agreed to go to his next match. "When is it?"

"I work here with you guys, so I just fight on weekends. This next weekend is a doozy too. I'm up against a guy way bigger than me who looks mean as a junkyard dog. Wait till you see him!"

"Wait a minute. I thought Golden Gloves did everything by weight classes."

"Usually they do but some of the fights aren't Golden Gloves. They usually have one before and after their fights that are uneven. It draws more people. I suppose the crowd likes to see the living hell kicked out of someone now and then"

When they arrived early for the fight, they saw the man Joe was going to fight. They were stunned. "You really gonna fight that monster?"

"Sure. Why not. People say he enjoys tuning up guys and pulping their faces, but I'm pretty fast. He's got to catch me to hurt me. I'm left-handed too. That used to be a problem. People always told me I was a dummy 'cause I couldn't do everything with my right hand. Well, boxing is different. They don't know how to fight a guy like me. My punches come in differently than they expect. That guy looks plenty tough though, so who knows? My boxing career could be really short. Here goes." He went into the locker room to get ready.

Joe came into the ring from one side and the "monster" came in from the other. They did their dance in the middle with the referee. The bell rang. Punches flew, some blood spattered, and both men went to their corners with the next bell. Joe was panting and bleeding, but the other guy just looked meaner. In fact, now he looked mad. The bell rang again—they bounced around some before the monster started battering Joe. It looked like he was going down. All Joe could do was keep his gloves up and try to stop the pummeling. Then the monster stepped back, still looking pretty fresh, while Joe was battered and bloody. He came at Joe again and swung his long punch, figuring his opponent was too tired and done-in to stop him. Joe was a swimmer before he started boxing, and he was fast. He dodged, flowed back in close and fast like he was pushing off a pool wall on a turn, swung his left glove with everything he had left and connected with the monster's jaw. The brute dropped like a sack of flour.

Joe was reenergized. The referee stood by him and counted off the seconds down for the monster. Then the ref scissored his arms above the defeated boxer and called out those words that made Joe feel like a million bucks. "Yer out! The winner, Joe Dewey!"

His friends went crazy. After Joe showered, the guys wanted to take him out drinking. Joe declined. He was a mess. "C'mon Joe, you put that beast in his place. A KO, man! Let's celebrate."

"Can't do it guys. Thanks for being here, but I think I broke my hand on that ox's jaw. My hands hurt a lot from fighting—that's why I have bandages on them sometimes at work. They keep a doc here for the fighters. I got to stick around and see him. Besides that, man, I got beat half to death. I'm feeling really lousy. Have a drink for me, okay?"

"Okay buddy, whatever you say. Let's go!"

Joe waited a long time to see the doc—an older, sweating man with just a light circle of hair around the edges of his skull. "I think I hurt my hand pretty bad, Doc."

"I expect you did. That guy was three years older than you, I'm guessing—that's using your real age, and he outweighed you by over fifty pounds. You're lucky to be standing. Let's see that hand." He looked both hands over closely, probing at them. "You're a lefty, aren't you, kid?"

"Yes sir."

"Well, that would be a great thing if your hands were bigger. Some fighters can't seem to adjust to a guy swinging strong left-handed punches. But..."

"But what?"

"Son, your hands are too small for boxing. There's no way you won't keep breaking your fingers and maybe both hands, but for sure your left, if you keep boxing."

"That's what the gloves are for, right?"

"No. The gloves are so your opponent doesn't push your brains through the back of your head. Your hands are just too small. Sorry."

That was when Joe realized he couldn't fight in the ring anymore.

The TVA had kind of played out for him, but it did get him out and on his own. After that, Joe moved around, finding jobs as he went.

Several years and four jobs later the war really did break out and it looked like the US finally would have to get into it at some point. The "War to End All Wars" didn't end war, so this was the next big fight, with a 2 added to it. Boys all over the country signed up, and a lot of young women too.

The minimum age was eighteen, and Joe was a young looking twenty-two.

He waited to enlist until the Axis Powers took Greece, and like hundreds of thousands of others, he signed up to fight for his country—everyone knew the Nazis were coming. He had gotten pretty good about lying about his age, but this time he didn't have to lie. He walked boldly into the recruitment center.

"I'm here to serve. Sign me up."

"How old are you kid?"

"Why does everyone ask me that? I'm twenty-two. Sign me up."

"Your folks okay with this?"

"Parents don't care. Sign me up."

"Pretty determined, aren't you?"

"Yep, sign me up."

"Okay kid, it's your life."

* * *

Basic training at Boot Camp was over for Joe before Pearl Harbor. He was surprised when his folks and his sister, Florence, and her husband Morton drove down to see him when he graduated from basic training. He was surprised they would come, and he was more surprised at how much it meant to him and how much he enjoyed them being there. After they left he was more homesick than he'd been in years.

When the USA entered the war his training was over and he was deemed fit and ready for combat. Boot camp was awful though, and lots of guys barely made it through. There was a war on, though, so almost everyone *did* make it through basic, even if barely.

They wallowed through mud, learning how to stay low as they crawled with their gear.

They ran obstacles, learning how to keep their heads down and not get killed by the live ammo being shot over them.

They built muscle as they ran for miles in full gear.

They stabbed dummies with bayonets, trying to learn how to hate and kill an enemy they'd never seen.

They learned how to shoot. Joe picked up some medals for how well he did.

All in all, it was a young man's game, and Joe did okay—he had stamina.

The Master Sergeant was well known to them all. He was sending them on to real duty now that he was done blistering them in training. "Listen up, you worms! If you're standing here right now you're probably alive. You all made it through, and now you'll find out what this war is all about. Not all of you will come home, either. But all of you *will* do your jobs and serve your country. So, you're all graduating from being worthless pieces of crap to being soldiers. Be proud of that and make me proud. Your assignments are on the board. Check them and be ready to move out tomorrow at zero six hundred. Transports will be in the compound! Dismissed!"

"I don't see us on there anywhere, Howard."

"We gotta be there, Joe. Keep looking."

"There's your listing. You're headed to France. Very cool, man, 'cause you can have all the wine you want. I hear that's all anybody drinks there."

"Hey, there's you, Joe! Oh man, you're really going to the far side of the world. You're going to Australia. By the time your boat gets there the war could be over." Both men laughed.

They walked back to barracks together. "France. You better watch out for the ladies, and not catch something you don't want to bring home."

"Yeah, right Joe. Like there won't be any chicks down under."

"I've heard Australia called that."

"No, man. I was talking about chicks in Australia being under you."

Both young men gave a feeble laugh as they felt their bravado slipping away—their imagined tours of duty were gaining substance and feeling all too real.

"Let's both be careful. And let's get in touch after the war and celebrate."

"Celebrate what?"

"I dunno. Whatever we'll have to celebrate, I guess."

"Livin' through it, maybe. That'd be a good thing."

Nobody caught any Zs that night. Tensions were high, and every conversation all night was about what might be over there, wherever each man was heading. A fair share of the talk was about each man's fear about not making it home again, although they all tried to put a brave face on their fears.

"What're you gonna miss the most, Joe?"

"I dunno. What about you?"

"I wish I'd married my girlfriend. I'd like to think of coming home to her and starting a family."

"Too late now."

"Yeah."

"What about you, Toad?" Toad's nickname came from his terrible complexion.

"I just wanted one more girl." He pursed his lips and closed his eyes.

"You mean, 'one girl, any girl.'"

"Yeah, well."

"Joe?"

"You know, I think I messed up. I wish I'd treated my dad and stepmom better. They're okay. I think I'll write them from Australia."

Toad laughed. "Nobody's gonna write nobody! We'll be too busy killing Nazis and Japs."

The small talk ended as most of them couldn't imagine killing someone else. The silence let a few drift off to sleep for a couple of hours.

It took almost three weeks for Joe's ship to make it to Australia. They had a couple of scares on the way, but the subs were US and allies, not Nazi. It was one of the calmest parts of the war for Joe.

DUSTY

I learned to hide in the woods and eat whatever I could find. It seemed like every day I might die, and every night when I found a place to hide and sleep, I was surprised. My life was made up of terrible times like that.

One day when I was hunting, Joe showed up with his friends. I followed them all day, and when they camped I sniffed all around them and stayed out of sight. I was quite good at being invisible after growing up alone and knowing I could be eaten if I wasn't careful.

I followed the four men for three days, and finally decided it would be worth the risk to meet them. As they played with some wire and stuff I didn't understand, I slowly crept up on them. I made some noise to make sure they'd hear me and not get spooked. Then Joe turned and saw me. He smiled at me; I didn't know it was a smile at the time—he showed his teeth but he didn't growl. It was a little confusing. He coaxed me closer, and I thought, Hey, too late now. I moved slowly into their camp. Joe reached out and touched me—I almost bit him. He scratched my ears, then lifted my chin. He looked into my eyes and said, "Man, what a dusty dog." He took his comb out of his pocket and brushed me down. Wow! That was really nice.

"I guess he's just a kind of dusty color, not white, but just off. Dusty—that's your name, boy." The other men were nice too. That was when I knew I didn't have to be alone anymore.

I learned a lot about them during the next three years while I trained them to give me parts of everything they ate. It was only right since we were a pack. Joe talked to the other men and to me about him growing up. I could tell it wasn't easy for him. Then I found out his name was Wilbur. I liked Joe better. I knew he did too, because once another man called him Wilbur, and laughed. Joe punched him.

HAZEL

She lived in the little town of Graham in western Kentucky, a town of six hundred people, many of whom worked in the coal mines. Youngest of eleven, she was the baby.

Her daddy was a huge coal miner, and her momma was a tiny woman who barely weighed a hundred pounds when she was nine months pregnant. Lelia had married Eli Stewart when she was twelve years old and had her first child before she was fourteen. She had babies for over twenty years, and all but one had lived. The other ten were married by the time Little Hazel was a teenager.

Her brother James was married to a Hazel, which made his wife Big Hazel. Little Hazel was the baby of the family, while Big Hazel was the already married woman. Size had absolutely nothing to do with it. To most everyone in the family they were Big Hazel and Little Hazel for the next eighty years.

Hazel's life was simple and rural. Everybody knew everybody else in town, but that didn't mean they all got along. She thought she had some "wild moments", but in reality her life was very calm and very much country. She did chores, went to school through the sixth grade, then helped out at home. Now and then she loved to go and stay with one or another of her married sisters. Some had young children of their own, so Hazel would help them out. Others had nearly grown kids, so some of Hazel's nieces and nephews were older than her.

Her tiny mama, Lela Stewart, was sitting in the porch swing, shucking beans, as Hazel plopped down next to her. "Momma, where did you get all my middle names? I hate my names."

"Why Hazel, your names are very nice. Why do you say that?"

"Well, I understand the "Arizona" name, because that's a state, but I don't know why it has to be *my* name. But my other middle name, Othella, that's just a bad name. I don't know anybody named Othella."

"We've had Othellas in the family, and it's a nice name. Don't you say anything like this to your daddy. He'll smack you into next week."

"I won't, but I hate my names. Hazel Arizona Othella Stewart is just a stupid name—a really long, stupid name."

Momma just smiled at her as she snapped beans on her apron. "Maybe, but it's all yours, honey. Besides, yours is not the longest name amongst our kids."

"Who has a longer one?"

"Your brother Gene. His whole name is Eugene Thomas Alonzo Jackson Stewart."

"Why so many?"

Lela laughed. "Well child, we had relatives expecting their names to show up in our family, so we put some of 'em in Gene's name."

"I guess it's better than 'Flossia.'"

"Now your sister likes her name just fine."

"You really think so? Then why does she go by 'Flossie?'"

"Well, it's hers, so it don't matter, either way." Mama just shrugged.

"And how come Vernie Mae never, ever goes by that? She's been Mae forever."

Lela stopped shucking and stared at her youngest. "You gonna poke fun at every name we chose for every child? Maybe Vernie wasn't the best choice, but it was ours, and that's the end of it."

"No Mama, sorry Mama."

When Hazel got into her teen years her friends were all dating, but she didn't date much. She really didn't have much in the way of nice clothes, and she didn't care much for most of the boys she knew. Her momma got married at twelve and had children for over twenty years. That wasn't part of Hazel's plan.

She did enjoy the popularity that came from being the prettiest girl in Muhlenberg County. Boys told her that often, and some adults said it too, so she believed it. She was a tease, but she was willing to wait for the right man.

Late in her teen years the war started. Even in their tiny coal town, young men enlisted or were recruited. Hazel had nothing to do but the boring stuff she always did.

She and her friend Peggy were talking about the war one day. "Haz, you should write some of those soldiers. You can get their addresses, you know, their army addresses, at the Army recruitment center over in Central City."

"What would I say?"

"Anything you want. You'll never meet 'em."

"Are you doin' it now?"

"Nah, but I think I'm gonna. Ask your folks; they'll think it's great."

"I think you're wrong about that, but it sounds like fun, so I'll try if you will."

"If they say yes, I'll get us to Central City for those cute soldier boys' addresses."

* * *

"Momma, you know it's okay. It's just letters. I mean, I'll never meet any of them, ever. The war's on the other side of the world."

"Ask your daddy. If he says it's alright, then it's alright with me, Li'l Hazel."

That night she did. Her daddy was rocking in the porch swing. It hung from the roof with chains, squeaking a bit as it swung slowly forward and back. Hazel talked fast as she made her case. "Daddy, I'm going to write some soldiers to make them feel like they got a USA home connection. I'll just write the ones overseas."

"Are you telling me, Li'l Hazel, or are you asking?"

"I guess I'm asking. It's okay, right?"

"No. Don't do it." He took his chewing gum out and stuck it in the chain that held up the swing, filling up another link with gum.

Hazel's eyes followed his movements. *He's about got that chain filled up with gum.*

"Daddy, I don't get it. You said we need to win this war, and the Nazi's is really bad people! Why cain't I write some soldiers and cheer 'em up?"

"No, Hazel. I won't have it. You're my baby, and I don't have to explain it to you. It's a bad idea. Drop it." He half raised his hand, which warned her off, then his hand kept reaching for a different, dried piece of gum stuck in the chain. He pried it off and popped it into his mouth. As she backed off a memory surfaced. *I remember when I was a little kid, sittin' at the supper table when different ones of my brothers got into arguments with Daddy. Even Gene. Course he was the oldest, and always in and out of trouble. He even carries a gun with him all the time. I remember Phutney stood up and yelled at Daddy, and fast as a cat jumpin' a mouse in the barn, Daddy hopped up, picked him up by his shirt and shook him like a hound shaking a squirrel. Poor skinny Phutney fell when daddy dropped him. He took a while gettin' up too. I don't want Daddy that mad at me.*

※ ※ ※

The next day she went over to Big Hazel's house. It wasn't much of a journey since it was only twenty feet from her door. Big Hazel married Little Hazel's brother, James, but everybody called him Phutney. "Hey Big Hazel, whatcha doin'?"

"Little Hazel, you scar't me to death, sneaking up on me like that. What are you doing here this time of day?"

"Well, you only live twenty feet from my house, so I thought I'd just come over and visit."

"Really? When was the last time you came over alone jest to visit?"

"Don't recall, but I'm here today."

"Well, I remember. Countin' today you've done it twice'st. That's how many times. So Haz, what is it you want to visit about? I can keep ironing, can't I?" She took her Dr. Pepper bottle with the funny sprinkler head on it and splattered the shirt with water. Then she put her hot iron to it—the water sizzled and steamed.

"Oh, I was thinking it would be a good thing to write some of those soldiers overseas, like the Simpson boy, Tim, and maybe Skinny Jones, that tall kid who graduated last year. Just to cheer them up you know."

"Why, that sounds like a nice thing to do. It would make them feel a little bit closer to home, and it would help you keep up with your writin' and penmanship, now that you're not in school."

Hazel pouted—a habit she had perfected. "That's what I thought, too. But Daddy and Momma don't want me to do it."

"Then why are you asking me about it? If they said 'no,' then it's no. Ain't it?"

Hazel stared at the rough wooden floor and started talking faster, like she was trying to convince herself. "The United States Post Office doesn't have age limits. I don't have to be any older to write letters. And the United States government wants us to help the war effort from home. We don't have any money, so we can't buy bonds, but I could write some soldiers. I could write a bunch of them boys."

"They're not boys. They're men, and I guess you could. But I won't lie to your folks for you. If they come right out and ask me if you're writing soldiers, I'll have to say 'yes'."

"But you think it's a good idea? And you won't tell Daddy if he don't ask?"

"That's right. Tain't none of my business. Don't be stupid now and tell your brother Phutney. He'd tell his daddy sure as shootin'. Come to think of it, he probably wouldn't think it's a very good idea either. He's a lot like his daddy, just smaller."

"Okay then. I got a bunch of them 3¢ stamps I had in school. They're each good for one letter. It'll be excitin' getting' letters from all over the world."

"I suppose it would be nice to hear from somebody outside of town now and then, come to think of it."

"Thanks Big Hazel." She rushed to the door. "Love you!"

Looking at the door her wispy little blonde namesake just ran through, Big Hazel sighed. *From this here start, I have to wonder what your life is gonna look like, girl.* Then she sprinkled some more water on a different shirt and kept on ironing.

* * *

"Okay Peggy. How do we get to Central City? I'm all set to do this."

"Really? Your folks were okay with it? Wow. That's great."

"I didn't say that. I said I'm ready to do it. I got the stamps and everything."

Peggy just rolled her eyes. She was used to her vivacious friend leaping into things she hadn't thought through. "This ain't like when we went out together with Jasper and Rooster, is it? When they brought out the beer you thought that was cool, but when that bottle broke and they started drinking it through pantyhose to strain the glass out, you got spooked. You took right off. I wasn't ready to go home, but you sure were. And that ruint the date."

"Nothin' like that, Peg. I swear."

"Alright. I'll talk Tony into taking us tomorrow. He can take us after work, and since he starts at five in the morning, he gets out at 2:30. His car can go anywhere. He keeps it up real good. He's the only guy I can think of with his own car that actually runs, and he's sweet on me. I'll have to reward him for this, you know." She had a wicked smile on her eighteen-year-old face.

"Peggy, you wouldn't!"

"Oh, I've let him feel me up lots of times. I haven't let him go any farther than that—yet." She laughed.

"Well, I made out with Ronny, the boy across the orchard from us."

"Didn't!"

"Did too!"

"When?"

"Well, it was a while ago."

Peggy laughed again. "It don't count if you kiss a boy when you're a kid, like ten years old. You done anything this year?"

Hazel looked down, deciding what to say. "Naw, I guess not. I'm waitin' for the right guy, that's all."

"Maybe some of them soldiers will come to Graham and show you a good time after they get out of the war." Peggy laughed, and Hazel punched her friend's arm, then laughed with her.

* * *

Hazel was good to her word. After they went to Central City and got a list of soldiers they could write, she started carefully writing letters. She wrote about staying safe, the weather, and anything she could think of. The letters weren't very long, but they were something for the boys to read. After she had six done, she rode her bike to their tiny post office to mail them.

"Hey there Li'l Hazel! You droppin' your folks mail off to go out?"

"No Mr. Snyder. This is my mail."

"Why, these are all going to an Army base. You writing soldiers to help with the war, young lady?"

"I am, but this is personal, right? You can't legally go and tell my parents I sent these, can you?"

"Well, that's not exactly right, but it don't hardly seem proper for me to tell somebody what anybody else does with the mail. This is a right of United States citizens. So, no Li'l Hazel, I won't say nothin' to nobody. Tic-a-lock." He smiled at her and made a motion at his lips like he was locking them with a key.

She grinned back and nodded, and with a deep sigh of relief, Hazel went her way.

* * *

It took three weeks to get her first reply. She had to go to the Graham Post Office every day so her letters wouldn't get delivered to her house. It just wouldn't do to have her daddy see them. Her first letter was from Sherman, a neighbor from a mile away. He asked about his folks and his dog. Then he wanted to know if she was still stealing apples from his folks' orchard. *Last letter you get, Sherman. That's just rude.* She didn't write him again.

The second reply came from a man she never met. He asked a lot of personal questions, like what she wore at night to bed and such. She decided he was a pervert and didn't write him back either.

The third and fourth letters took a whole month. They were also from guys she didn't know—Randy Smith and Joe Dewey. She'd gotten their names from her mother's sisters in Michigan.

Aunt Lucy sent her Randy's name and address. Her husband Jim worked in the car factory in Pontiac, and they knew about this soldier because Uncle Jim knew his dad from the shop.

Aunt Noni was her momma's other sister who moved to Michigan. She and her husband, Claude, moved for the same reason everybody did—to get a good job in the car factory. They left the wide-open spaces of Kentucky, but Kentucky never left them. They finally bought a farm, and now and again her momma got a letter from Noni.

Randy lived in Michigan when he wasn't fighting the war. He talked about snow and winter and how much he missed it, since it was so hot and all over there. She wrote him a nice letter about the weather in Graham, Kentucky. It was the only weather she'd ever known.

Let's see what that other Michigander, Joe, has to say. She tore it open and there were two pictures and a letter. She took a long time studying the pictures before she read his letter. *He seems like a nice man and he's got a dog in the war. I wonder how that happened? It's a good picture he sent of him and Dusty. He's a good-lookin' man. I believe I'll send him a picture of me.*

She read his letter a bunch of times. *I'd recognize him anywhere now that I've stared at his pictures a thousand times. Look at those muscles, and that's the cutest crew cut. Joe Dewey...hmmm.*

He wrote about how hot it was and asked if it was hot in Kentucky now. He asked about her family, and that opened a big topic for her to write about. She had ten brothers and sisters, and all those brothers and sisters-in law. She wrote him that night, and mailed it the next day, along with her reply to the letter from the other Michigan guy, Randy. She had to force herself to finish that one.

* * *

"So, any new letters, Haz?"

"Oh yeah, Peggy. I'm gonna marry this one."

"Oh, you ain't. You'll never even meet him. Don't be silly. This is just pen-pal stuff."

"Don't you believe it. He's got a big white dog he named Dusty. He's half dingo, you know, a wild dog there in Australia. I'm going to write him every day till the war is over."

"No you're not. You'll forget all about it. I'm going to write the fellas I started with again, but that's all. It takes too much time, and them three-cent stamps, well, you gotta pay for 'em somehow!"

"I'm gonna bag groceries and help sweep up on weekends at Mr. Featherston's store. His boy Gary doesn't want to work so much, so I can help out. I'm eighteen now, so Daddy doesn't mind if I work for some spending money. He's gonna pay me 10¢ an hour. That'll buy a lot of stamps. Anything so I can keep writing Joe. He's coming down here after the war and marryin' me. And that's just it."

"Did he tell you that in his letter?"

"No, not yet. But he will." Hazel pulled out her latest letter from Joe. She showed Peggy the envelope, which had her big, red, lipstick kisses on the back, and on the front she'd written just above the address to Miss Hazel Stewart, in pencil, *Mrs. Hazel Dewey*. "This is what I expect will happen!"

Free
ARMY POSTAL SERVICE
JUN 25 1945
A.P.O.
Miss. Hazel Stewart
Graham, Kentucky
U.S.A.
PASSED BY
16165
EXAMINER

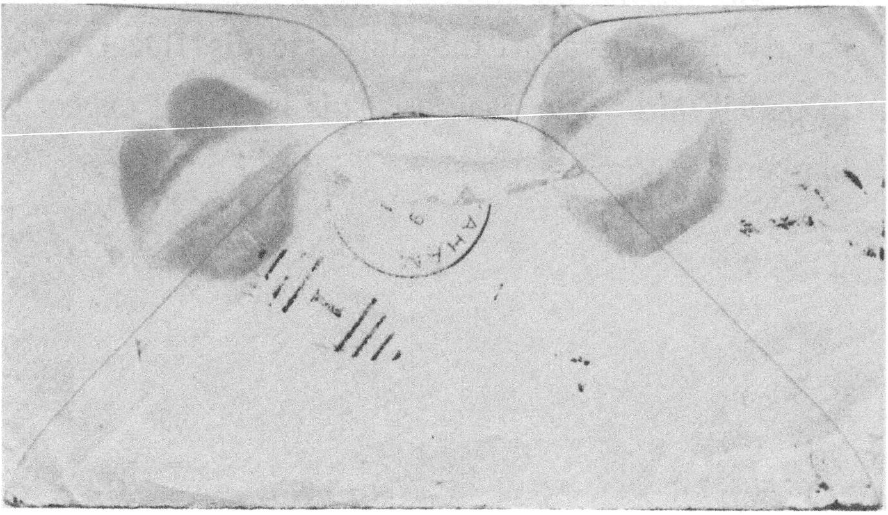

"Hey, show me the pictures you said he sent you. Don't hold out on me, now."

Hazel laughed. "Okay, here they are." She pulled them out of her book.

"Ooh, he is a hottie. Wonder why he sent a picture of himself with no shirt on, huh?" She poked Hazel and laughed.

"I'm sending him a picture of me in my next letter."

"Which one?"

"Best one I got. I don't have many, but the one I got done with my hair all fluffy is the best."

Hazel's plan to trap this young soldier went well for the next dozen or so letters. They slowly turned to letters that said things like, "I love to get your letters. They make my day in this awful place." They were signed, "Love, Joe." Her letters were very similar. She didn't remember who wrote about love first, but she was sure it must have been him.

When he told her the story of Dusty saving him and his three buddies, she had to tell all her friends in town. They told other people, and after some thirty people were keeping her secret, somebody told her daddy. When thirty people are keeping a secret, it's not a secret.

Eli was sitting by the back door when she walked into the house before supper. "Hi Daddy. How's your day going?"

"Well, after I worked underground with a pick and shovel for nine hours, then pumped up the leaky tire on the Model A and cranked it up and drove home, I heard my little girl was writing soldiers. You got any thoughts about that?"

'Sorry Daddy. I decided it was the right thing to do, and now they depend on my letters."

His voice was as calm and gentle as ever. "It was the wrong thing to do. Do you know why?"

She answered in a tiny voice her daddy could barely hear. "No. Why?"

He bellowed it out. "Because you *asked* me, and I told you NO!"

"I'm sorry I disobeyed, Daddy, but I'm pretty gown up now. I figured I could do what I decided was right."

He reached out for her with his blackened hands, dark from deep-mine coal dust, and she cringed back. He grabbed her and hugged her close. "I'm sorry too. I'm sorry you did it, but it's done. You started this, so it's yours now. Don't do anything too stupid, girl." He held her for a long moment and patted her back with his big hands. Then he kissed the top of her head and let her go.

She didn't remember a hug like that from him before. She figured he was all hugged out after the first ten kids. It was a moment she would always treasure. She started to get up and Eli surprised her.

"Baby girl, let's go sit on the side porch and swing for awhile. That be okay?"

"Sure Daddy. That would be nice."

They walked the short distance and sat in the swing. Eli started it moving and reached for a dry piece of gum from the chain. "Want some?"

"Laud'a'mercy, Daddy, no. I prefer new gum."

"Sure, if you got it. I don't, so this will do."

They sat and shared the quiet comfort of the swing, quietly putting the tension to rest.

DUSTY AND JOE

When I met Joe and his buddies their pack seemed big to me since I was alone. Joe smelled right. I knew he was okay, and I decided he was mine. He smelled right, and when I licked him it felt right. He rubbed my ears a lot and brushed me, and that felt right.

The others were okay. They let me stay with them and travel through the jungle with them. I brought them an occasional rabbit and some other things I caught. They only ate the rabbits, not the mice and bush rats. My rabbits were a lot better than the stuff they fed me from cans that didn't smell real.

Mostly we went from place to place and put down wire. Sometimes I had to stay way back while they helped fire big things that made a BOOM sound. The booming was pretty scary. Joe can tell the story of how I saved them.

* * *

The Japanese held the Philippine Islands for four years. They had a strategic air and naval base there, and Douglas MacArthur determined they had to be driven off the islands.

The camp commander approached Joe and Dusty, who was always by his side. "Joe, what do you want to do with Dusty on this new campaign? You know it won't be here in Australia."

"Sir. I thought about it, and I guess, if command allows it, I think he should be with me no matter where that is. He really does function with our squad. He's our scout. Dusty stays ahead of us and lets us know if anybody is in the area. He doesn't miss much."

"Your girl back home know about Dusty?"

"Oh yes sir! She's told everybody around there about him too. I sent her some pictures of Dusty and me. We've never actually met, but we've been writing and I plan to marry her when I get home."

"Haven't met her, huh? Quite a story. I wish you and Dusty the best with that. He deserves a good home with people who love him."

The CO's love of dogs was obvious. He squatted down by Dusty and encouraged him to come to him. The dog stood and walked to him, sat down and waited. The CO spoke directly to him, playing with the dogs pointed ears as he spoke. "What do you think boy? Do you want a break from the war, or do you want to stay with Joe?"

Dusty sat on his haunches staring at the CO for a few seconds. Then he licked his face and moved back to sit beside Joe again.

The CO stood. "I guess that's it. He wants to go with you. Well, he's smarter and better trained than these grunts. He'll be fine." His gaze swept the camp, encompassing the soldiers scrambling to get ready for the offensive. "Take care of this animal, Sergeant."

Joe returned his salute. "Yes sir!"

* * *

They were transported by boat to Luzon in the Philippine Islands the next morning. They arrived at the makeshift camp that was the headquarters of the new offensive. A Master Sergeant was waiting to meet the new troops.

"'Tenshun!"

Ranks were immediately formed. Dusty sat on his haunches between Joe and Bob, another man in his squad. The Master Sergeant paced in front of them. He stopped in front of Bob. "Soldier, what the hell is this?"

"Sir?"

"This animal by you is what. What's it doing here?"

Bob was unprepared to face down the Master Sergeant. "Sir, he's Sergeant Dewey's partner." He indicated Joe, standing at attention beside him. The Master Sergeant took a step sideways. He had the same mean, practiced stare shared by every Master Sergeant. "Well?"

"Sir, Dusty has an unofficial rank of First Private, and he's our scout. Our CO approved him coming with us."

"Your CO? What's his name—Mary?"

"Sir, I sense you disapprove of Dusty."

"Do you, now? Very perceptive. If you haven't noticed, nobody else brought their pet with them."

"Sir, my point is that Dusty defends our squad, in the field and in camp. He doesn't know you and I think I should point out that he's ready to defend us again." Joe looked down at Dusty, who had started an ominous growl deep in his throat.

The Master Sergeant looked down at the moderately angry dog. "Always defends you guys, huh?"

"Yes sir. We figured he'd be our scout again as we lay down wire for communications ahead of our troops."

"I know what your job is, mister!" The fearless Master Sergeant dropped instantly to one knee in front of Dusty. "That so, dog?"

Dusty barred his fangs at the man in front of him but didn't move an inch. Master Sergeant stayed on his knee and angled his head up to face Joe. "Will he attack me?"

"Only if I tell him to, sir, or if you hit me."

With no effort and a startling grace for his hard-toned bulk, he stood and faced Joe. "Good enough. Take care of each other.

"Listen up, you morons! Our job is to push the Japs back. Got it? You'll each be part of a team—stay with that team. Keep to your map. Keep moving north. The dog," he glanced at Dusty, "and his team will be laying down wire for communications. Until they get it done you're on your own. If you get in trouble, hide or start back. We have a team to contact you when we've gone far enough. That's why it's important for you to stay on location. If you don't, we can't find you. We move out in four hours. Get ready. Dismissed!" He turned to Joe's squad. "You've got your instructions and your equipment. Dusty, move your team out!"

Master Sergeant turned to walk away, paced by his second. "Sir, that was, ah, surprising."

"Shut up. I'd give my right arm for a dog in this hell hole."

* * *

A mile into the jungle Bob laughed out loud. "What?"

"Well, the Master Sergeant put Dusty in charge. I just find that hilarious since he started out challenging his right to be here at all."

Joe held up his fist to stop their movement. They waited silently. "Alright. Dusty's in charge. He'll give orders through me, got it?"

They all laughed. "No more talking. This jungle is crawling with Japs. Let's do our jobs and get out. Hazel will be seriously put out if you guys get me killed."

With quiet chuckles they moved on, keeping some jungle between them and inhabited villages.

They were taking it slow, but Dusty always had so much energy he would often race ahead. He never went too far before heading back. They were unrolling wire and moving slowly when he did one of his sprints. He took off and in a flash was fifteen feet down the trail from them. He hit the landline at a run and triggered the explosion. He dropped to the ground immediately. The explosion threw the four men in different directions—everybody hit the ground. They were farther away from the explosion than Dusty, so he took the brunt of the damage.

Guys started picking themselves up. "I can't see anything!"

"Give it a minute, Bob! Check for broken bones and cuts."

"It's okay. It's just blood in my eyes."

"Dusty!" Joe scrambled up and raced for the dog. "Oh man, he's hurt real bad.

"C'mon guys. We've got to go back to camp. Dusty needs some fixing." The guys gathered around, Joe picked Dusty up and carried him as they made their way back to their small, crude campsite.

After they got to their one-night camp they dressed Dusty's cuts, bandaged the end of what was left of his tail, and splinted his leg. "Man, he's not gonna like that splint. We can't let him walk for a couple of weeks, guys."

"But Joe, we've got to finish up this line. We're in the middle of a campaign—men will die if we don't get it done."

"I know that. Of course we have to finish. We'll just have to take him with us. If it was your leg that was broke we wouldn't leave you here either—at least I don't think we would. We'd probably have to take a vote." They cut two long sticks, tied some canvas to them and dragged it behind them as they moved along the jungle paths—they couldn't stay in one place for two weeks. It would be too dangerous for them and the guys who depended on them for a line of communication. Dusty didn't look too comfortable being dragged on a travois, but he had a broken leg, so he didn't fight it.

The men had suffered some cuts and bruises, but they were minor, so they healed up as they worked. They finished up in the Philippines and were shipped back to Australia. Things went back to what passed as "normal" for them, except for Dusty. The squad hit the trails again but had to leave Dusty there till he healed. Unfortunately, that meant he had to stay at camp with men who weren't part of his pack. Dusty got mean at times because he didn't know them as well. He knew the CO.

The CO stopped by regularly to check on Dusty. He always brought some broken cookies and some meat scraps. He'd sit and talk with Dusty and tell him Joe was okay. He just enjoyed spending time with the dog. On one visit a jeep chugged by as he was feeding Dusty cookies.

Dusty tore out the screened doorway and chased after the jeep.

The CO ran madly after him, forgetting all rank and decorum. When he caught up the driver was unsuccessfully trying to talk Dusty down.

"Dusty, down!" To the COs surprise Dusty dropped to his haunches and sat quietly.

"Wow. How'd you get him to do that, sir?"

"I'm the CO. He knows that. Dusty, c'mon." The CO grinned to himself as he and his charge went back to the cook's tent. He looked at Dusty. "I think your leg is pretty well healed."

Soon after that he went on patrol with his squad again, and things got back to as normal a routine as war allows.

For weeks at a time they had no assignment, so they helped with the hot, sweaty work of maintaining the camp. They were quite close to the ocean, so they went swimming whenever they could. Dusty loved the ocean. Joe didn't care for it as much, but swam anyway. He mentioned it in one of his letters to Hazel.

3.

got much to do. We are only about 300 yards from the ocean so I take Dusty down whenever I get a chance. The waves are usually so big that he has a rough time and so do I sometimes. Its fun swiming in the ocean but I would lots rather swim in fresh water. The ocean is to rough to swim. All you can do is play around and splash in the waves.

    I better close now honey because I have ran out of words and I want to write a few lines to the folks before it gets to late.

All My Love,
Joe

Joe kept his unit tight as they crept past enemy lines and strung their communication wire for the phones. Dusty and his squad were known to everybody there. New soldiers quickly figured out he was part of Joe's squad. For three years the four men and Dusty functioned as a unit. Dusty was part of his pack of five, but he usually got along pretty well with the other men in camp.

Joe heard the laughter start as a jeep drove through camp, honking. Then he heard Dusty barking like a demon-dog. He ran halfway across the camp to get to the scene where Dusty had treed a jeep. At least, Dusty thought so. He loved to chase every vehicle that came into camp. This particular jeep stopped after Dusty chased it halfway through the camp. The driver was from another unit and didn't know Dusty. He was standing up in the seat kicking at the apparently vicious dog trying to climb through the side of the vehicle.

"Dusty, down!" The dog promptly sat with his tongue lolling out and stared at the nervous driver. "You can get down from that seat, soldier. Dusty won't hurt you. He just likes to challenge jeeps. I see he won this time."

"Sargent, yes sir!" The newcomer looked down at the now calm dog and grinned. "He does seem to think he won the fight."

"He'd never hurt you, but thanks for giving him a run. Let's get you to the captain."

Dusty escorted the two men the short distance to the captain's tent.

∗ ∗ ∗

Snags leap out at times when least expected.

Snags can often change everything.

This snag was the transfer of their CO who loved dogs. The new guy clearly did not share that love.

The new captain stopped Joe as his unit returned from patrol. He had just arrived a couple of weeks earlier and hadn't had time yet to get to know his men. "Dewey, I've seen you and your men take your dog on patrol, but I'm here to tell you to get rid of that dog. He's not a trained Army Canine and there's no place for him in this camp. Just yesterday he endangered a currier in his jeep." The captain looked down at Dusty, whose tongue was hanging out the side of his mouth as he stared at this new man who wasn't being friendly to Joe. He cocked his head sideways.

"No sir, he did not, and I can't do that."

"Soldier, that's not a request. Get rid of the dog."

"No sir, I still can't do that."

"What do you mean, you can't? Do it! We don't keep pets in the Army, and you know it! Do you see anyone else with a dog, or any pussycats around the base? Of course not. We don't keep pets!"

Dusty started growling. *This man shouldn't yell at Joe.*

"Can't do it sir. Dusty saved my life and the lives of my squad. Four United States soldiers owe him their lives. Can't do that to him."

"Then I'll get rid of him for you! Get out of my way."

"No sir, I can't let you do that either. You'll have to go through me to get to Dusty." Joe knew this was going to be a problem, but there wasn't time to stop and consider consequences. "Dusty's *my* dog, and nobody's taking him away." The captain pushed him to move him aside—that's when he slugged his captain in the gut and followed up with a left cross to his jaw.

One of Joe's buddies was holding me and keeping me from the bad man. Once Joe hit him I tore loose and was on the captain before he knew he was on the ground. I growled as I gripped his throat. I looked to Joe and waited.

"Dusty, no! Let go, now! You can't stay with me if you rip his throat out. He's not making you leave, boy. Are you, Captain? Let him up, Dusty."

The captain got up fast, shaking his head to clear the fog, not so sure about keeping the fight going. "Sorry sir, but Dusty saved four soldiers and deserves better than being tossed out like yesterday's rations. He does, and if I'm in trouble for standing up for him, so be it. He stood up for me and saved my life. And he seems pretty well trained to me, sir, but it does look like he just takes orders from me."

"Damn Dewey, you nearly broke my jaw. I heard you boxed Golden Gloves. I'm guessing you were pretty good."

"Had to quit sir. I kept breaking bones in my fingers. My hands are too small." He paused for a few seconds. "But I can still fight." He stood there flexing his hands, ready to defend himself and Dusty.

"All right, you're a good soldier, and I'll concede about the dog. He did save your lives, and that counts for something. You're going on report for striking an officer, but that's all. I won't push it and I won't press charges this time."

"Dusty?"

"He's yours soldier, and I guess you're our unit's GI Joe. Keep Dusty out of trouble."

"Hell sir, Dusty's smarter than most of the guys in camp."

"Don't know if that means he's a smart dog or that these butt-ugly grunts are dumber than rocks, but okay. He's your dog. You know you're not taking him back to the States, right?"

"Guys take guns and trophies back all the time. Dusty's kind of both. I'll work it out Sir. My girl in Kentucky is really wanting to meet Dusty, so I have to get him home."

"You can try, soldier, you can try."

Joe dropped to his knees and gave me a hug. That was when I knew Joe was mine forever. His hand was bleeding from punching the bad man, so I licked it.

* * *

Australia didn't see much actual conflict. There were Japanese squads circulating, and fighting certainly occurred, but it wasn't a major site of engagements. New Guinea, however, was close and the Japanese had built up a large air and naval base. It was a perfect place from which to launch attacks on Australia and was key to holding the Philippines.

Some action in New Guinea is recorded history, and some was not recorded. The US wasn't supposed to send so many troops there with the Australian army, but they did, and some of it was classified. Some men never spoke of it, even when they got home.

Joe was sitting on his bunk with his pad turned so the top of the letter was facing his chest. He was writing a note to Hazel. As he wrote he kept wiping sweat off so it wouldn't blur the pencil-written letter on the pulpy paper. He looked up when he heard the call to formation. His buddy, Bob, ran up to the tent. "C'mon, Joe! We're getting sent someplace!"

"On my way Bob." He wrote a final sentence to Hazel and signed it, "*Love, Joe.*"

Joe's squad got their first orders to ship out to New Guinea. "Men, it's a quick ride to New Guinea, and it's absolutely essential for the Pacific Theatre to stop the Japs there. You specialists will be placing wire for our communications in the field. Unfortunately, we don't have the area yet, so it's enemy territory until the job is done.

"Also, you will speak to no one about this and write to no one at home about it. This is a top-secret mission. Most of the troops there will be Aussies, but our tech teams will make a big difference. You leave at zero two hundred. Dismissed. Dewey, remain behind."

"Sir!"

"I'm sorry, Joe. Dusty has definitely proven his worth, but he has to sit this one out. Cook says he can stay with him like he did when he was hurt."

Joe didn't have time to write Hazel about the combat mission in the brief time before they left. Once in the boat, though, he pulled out his pad and pencil and started writing. Bob watched him with some amusement.

"Joe, you won't get to mail that until we're back. What's the point?"

"Heading out to combat like this is a big deal, so I want to tell her about it. I'll hand it off to someone to mail for me who isn't landing, like the driver of this boat."

He wanted to tell her about it, but he couldn't disobey orders. Besides, he knew they checked some mail, and it might not get through if he mentioned New Guinea.

Darling Hazel:

Here goes another short letter honey but it will have to do for now. I'm on a boat and heading for combat but I can't tell you anymore about it. I didn't think I would get a chance to write for awhile but I did so I'm just writing a few letters while I have a chance. I cant tell you where I'm going but dont worry because I will be alright and I will write you as soon as I can after I get there.

All My Love,
Joe

He included a picture from a different location he already had developed.

Hazel thought about that letter for a long time. *I'm gonna send him another picture, but a smaller one he can keep with him on the combat missions he goes on. This one isn't my best, with all the lines in it from the cheap paper, but it's okay. He may get it wet or smashed up or something since he'll take it with him to the fightin'.*

Joe's squad and one other were packed in the transport ship with a mass of Australian troops. "Remember guys, when we hit the beach, our job is not to engage the enemy, but to get to the woods and head due north. Try to stay in sight of each other, but do not, I repeat, do not mix in with the Australian assault troops. Got it?"

His squad nodded, nervous at being with assault troops. Their job was usually to slip past and hide as they set up communications networks. Despite the combat they'd seen, this was all new.

Hundreds of men hit the beach at a run, carrying all their gear on their backs. Joe's squad, along with two Aussie troopers assigned to help them, had a heavy load, with rolls of wire and tools, along with their regular combat packs. Six of them started up the beach to the woods—five made it.

The five stopped just inside the tree line. As Sergeant, Joe was in charge. After a quick head count, he looked back and saw their sixth man lying on the beach. "Think we can get him?"

The remaining Australian nodded no. "I saw him go down. The rounds went straight through and tore his chest apart. He's gone. Let's keep going."

"Everyone else okay?"

Several answered yes. Fred hesitated. "I think, hmm."

"What, Fred?"

"I was hit, I guess. Seems like just a graze though. We can check it out later. It burns, but I'm alright."

"You're sure?"

"Absolutely. And I'm not crossing that beach again to get to a boat. I'll stay with you guys."

"Okay guys, move out."

The first three days were hell. Japanese soldiers attacked with guns, swords, grenades, and eerie noises at night. One enemy soldier crept up to the edge of the camp in absolute silence. Joe only saw him by accident when he slowly stood up behind one of Joe's guys to quietly slit his throat. Joe had been fiddling with his sidearm at the time, raised it calm as could be, and fired. Everyone jumped, scared to death. As the Jap soldier went down they realized what was going on.

"We're up—stay up. Nobody sleeps tonight. You two, walk the perimeter. Let's not have any more surprises." Joe seemed calm as could be as he gave orders. He walked to the man he shot and saw the hole in his chest with a dark, wet pattern spreading around it. "This guy's a kid. What a war."

Then he walked away and threw up. From that night on they used extreme caution and still had constant problems. Not a man in the squad came back from that trip unscathed, and not all came back. Their one Australian trooper was exceptional. Without him they'd never have made it back. He recognized traps, heard things they couldn't hear, and was ruthless when necessary.

One night Joe's squad was crawling through the mud when mortar shells started hitting the area. They all hunkered down to wait it out—real cover was too far away.

Joe tended to be methodical. He stared at his watch until the shelling stopped. He didn't move. Ten minutes later he looked up from his watch. "All clear!" They started moving again. He kept track of everyone and realized right away Buck wasn't moving.

"Bob, let's check on Buck. You two, keep going. We'll catch up."

They moved to Buck's position—it was clear what happened even before they got there.

"Roll him over."

"You sure? Look at his head; it ain't right."

"No choice. Roll him." Bob and Joe both gagged when they saw his forehead and the top of his skull were gone.

The two men decided crawling through the mud was unnecessary since the shelling had stopped, so they lifted

Buck's body and carried him to the other guys and pulled his dog tags. They made a note of where they left him and kept moving.

Joe never spoke of the horrors he'd seen in New Guinea to his dad, stepmom or his kids, later in life. Hazel knew most of it, but not until years later. He couldn't keep it from her. One night he started punching their headboard while he was asleep. It terrified Hazel, but she took some water she kept by the bed and splashed him. He woke up and realized what he was doing.

He spent the rest of the night telling her about his experiences and nightmares. He never spoke about being in New Guinea or the Philippines. It was a time he never wanted to think about again.

10,000 MILE COURTSHIP

Hazel wrote several men in different branches of the military. She dropped most of the others after Joes letters got personal and ended with, *Love, Joe.* She kept up with one other army guy and a sailor. They were nice enough, and she liked getting the mail. She even mentioned them to Joe in her letters to him.

Joe got his first letter from Hazel Stewart in Graham, Kentucky, after he'd been in Australia for a few months. Her letter was nice, but not very personal. But still, it was a letter from home, and home was 10,000 miles away right now. He decided, even while he was reading it, that he would write back to her.

They corresponded for a few months and the letters became frequent. Then one day Joe signed his letter to her, "*Love, Joe.*"

Her next three letters got to him before she got that one—the fourth letter was signed,

"*I love you too,*

Hazel."

He sometimes sat for long minutes trying to think of something to say in the letter he was trying to write at the moment.

It often came out like this one.

April 4, 44

Dearest Hazel,

Its 10:60 P.M. and raining and I am tired and dirty but I guess I will write you a letter before I wash and go to bed. I know I would go to sleep if I started writing after I get cleaned up. I was going to write to you this morning but I didn't get a chance. I wanted to get a letter from you today too but I didn't so maybe I will get one tomorrow. If I do I will be able to think of more to write.

Its raining harder now and rain on the roof always makes me sleepy. I guess Dusty is sleepy too. He got well and he just curled up and I think he is asleep already. He sleeps all the time anyway.

Well Hazel darling I know that this is a very short letter but I guess you can excuse me this time. Its time for the light to be turned out anyway so I will have to close.

All My Love —
And Kisses Joe

Sometimes Joe had something serious to say, so he took his time wording it to make it just right. Sometimes he took more than one day to write it.

Getting to Kentucky to meet Hazel was the most important thing on his mind, and he wanted to make the right decision. He wrote to her about having to choose between a furlough, which would mean a chance to see her sooner, but then a return to combat, or staying the course and waiting for his rotation out of the action, and probably the war. He wanted to know what she thought.

May 9th

Darling Hazel;
    Its hot again today sweetheart and I feel like I'm going to melt. I wish it would rain and cool things off a little.
    Honey I have a problem to figure out and I cant quite decide what to do. I dont know wheather to come home on a furlough or wait for rotation. If I come home on a furlough I will have to come back but if I wait for rotation

I wont and I might be discharged when I get home because they are going to let some men out that have long overseas service. I think I could get a furlough next month but I think it would be best not to take it. I dont like the thought of coming back here again. I wanted to get home this summer ~~~~ to see you but maybe I will yet if things go right.

    I hope you think of me when you wear this locket I am sending and dont forget

               I love you,
              Joe

Dearest Joe,

I'm trying to be patient, but I'm not so good at it. I want you here as soon as you can be, but I understand about not going back. I don't want you to go back again either. It would break my heart to have you leave again once you get here. You will have enough points soon and I can wait that long – I guess.

It's still hot here. Summer is full on now, so everyone will sweat until fall.

Stay cool if you can at all.

   Love,

   Hazel

He resolved the furlough and rotation issue in his mind and wrote Hazel about it. Then the system changed. He knew she hadn't even gotten his letter yet, but the time problem was something he didn't think much about. He wrote and mailed letters when he could.

Hmm, I'm correcting something I wrote to her that she hasn't even seen yet. Well, she'll get the first letter about rotation first, even if it's in two weeks, then this one. Either way she'll know what the problem is for me. I'll write her again right away and explain it to her. I sure hope she doesn't get this letter first, somehow.

May 20

Darling Hazel,
 It seems like something always changes right after I write you a letter. Right after I wrote the last letter they stopped rotation and now are using a point system which you have probably heard about already. We get a point for each month in the army and one for each month we have been overseas and I get five points for each star and I have five stars so altogether I have 112 points. I have more points then most of the men over here but I still dont know when I will get home but I dont think

it will be very long. I've been telling you that so long now that you probably get tired of hearing it and I dont blame you. I sure will be glad when I can tell you that I am on the way home. I want to come home so bad that I'm liable to get grey hair from thinking about it. I keep thinking about all the things I'm going to do and darling I have some nice things planned and I sure hope they work out like I want them to. There is one main thing that I have planned but I dont think I should say any thing about it until I get home.

Joe wasn't so pleased she kept up with any other soldiers. She dropped her pen-pals one at a time until the only other man she was corresponding with was a sailor. Joe was clear about his feelings on the matter in one of his many letters.

There was humor at times in their letters. Hazel had mentioned a phrase that was a play on words about Kentucky's well known fast horses and beautiful women. He responded in his next letter with humor, and an absolute honesty regarding his jealousy.

April 27

Dearest Darling,
    I got two letters from you today honey and sure was glad to get them. The fellows around here say my eyes light up every time I get a letter from you. Maybe they do because it sure makes me happy. I also got a letter from you yesterday. I'm getting a little behind so I guess I'll have to see if I can get caught up. The trouble is trying to think of something to say. I could keep saying I love you but maybe I have said it to much already but I'll keep on saying it until I get there and

then I'll tell you again.

I almost wish you hadn't told me about that sailor who writes to you because it kind of worries me. I never knew I could be jealous but I guess I am.

Yes darling I have heard the expression about Ky's fast women and beautiful horses and I hope the part about the fast women it true when I get to your place.

From now on I'll see if I can write every other day or maybe every day if I get a chance and maybe I can get caught up a little. I hope you dont get tired of hearing from me if I write to often.

Love and Kisses
Joe

Joe kept none of Hazel's letters to him during the war. He was a guy, and just didn't think in terms of keeping things like letters. It was too difficult getting everything ready to go back to the States, along with fighting for Dusty to come with him.

Hazel, however, kept all her letters from him. Later she destroyed many which were too personal for her to ever risk someone finding. She kept this one because she liked to remind herself Joe got jealous, and she kept a few others which were dear to her, but not too revealing. The sailor, however, never got another letter from her.

Their letters turned to their ultimate meeting. Hazel had written she wanted them to meet—together and alone *before* he came to her parents' house. Some private time sounded good to Joe, but he was pretty sure it would be tough or impossible.

Ultimately, they weren't able to manage a meeting before he arrived at her parents' home. The lack of a telephone in her home or any neighbors was too great an obstacle.

He would have to meet her for the first time with her parents watching.

July 8th
Luzon, P.I.

Darling Hazel;
 I received a very sweet letter from you today honey and I will try to answer it but I wrote to you yesterday so I probably wont be able to think of much to say. You said you wanted to meet me someplace before we went to your house. Thats alright with me because I would rather not have any body else around when I see you. I dont know very much about Graham though so you will have to tell me where to meet you and then I'll let you know when I'll be there.

2.

Darling if some one around there had a phone I would call you when I get to the States and then I could tell you just when I would be in Graham. If you dont have a phone I'll write you as soon as I get there.

We are having very nice weather today. The wind is blowing through our tent and nearly taking the tent with it. I would sure like to be home in weather like this. We could have a lot of fun.

Its about 4 hours later now honey because I quit writing for awhile and went down to the ocean for a swim. Its sunday and I havent

They mostly wrote about everyday, ordinary things. Joe talked about swimming in the ocean whenever he and Dusty could, and how hot and humid it was all the time. He wrote about how he didn't have anything to write about, but then he wrote anyway.

Hazel, in turn, talked about her family, wanting to be with him, and the weather.

One thing they both wrote to each other in every letter was their love.

END OF THE WAR

Joe found himself terrified as his time in combat neared an end. Terrible thoughts kept swirling through his head.

What if I never meet Hazel? I'm so close to getting out and starting a life with her. I could die on my next patrol and we'd never meet.

The war wound down and guys were getting discharged right and left. Joe's squad was mustered out in September of '45. They stood around talking, not willing to walk away to their separate paths. They had depended on each other to survive—that built a special bond. It was their last time together—they never met as a group again. They mostly spoke of shipping out and what that meant.

Bob brought up the subject of their fifth squad member, Dusty. "Joe, we all think Dusty should go home with you.

We'll keep in touch, but like you told the captain when you thumped him, Dusty's your dog. If you get home and need anything for him, ever, you let us know and we'll take care of it."

"Thanks guys. That means a lot. Man, I don't know what I'd do without him. Gonna miss you guys something awful."

"Bring it in, GI Joe. Dusty too." Each man hugged, then dropped to give Dusty a goodbye hug, and walked away toward their uncharted, post-war lives.

* * *

Joe shipped out and was discharged in Detroit, Michigan, on September 20th, 1945. He'd gone in there since he was from Pontiac, just thirty miles north.

"C'mon Dusty. I saved most of my money the past year, so let's buy a car and go marry Hazel. I've got $945 in my pocket from my mustering out pay. Let's go spend some of it."

First Joe called ahead to let his family know when he'd show up. Then he dickered with the used car dealer, and finally ended up with what he believed to be a decent used car. He threw his duffle in the back seat and held the door for Dusty. Then he headed for the place he no longer considered home. His folks lived there, but he didn't.

When he pulled in there was a small crowd. His older sister, Florence and her husband Morton was there, along with his little sister, Serena. He gave them both big hugs. He swung tiny Serena around in the air. "Sis, I thought you'd keep growing, but I guess I was wrong." They both laughed.

Despite all the times he ran away, problems with his folks and still not wanting to live with them, he was glad to be back. He and his dad gave each other solid, emotional hugs. Mildred was there to welcome her stepson home with tears in her eyes.

Stuart cornered his son during the festivities. "Son, your sister Florence did some work on some of what happened over there with you and Dusty. She sent your picture and an article to the Pontiac Daily Press about it."

"Really? They do anything with it?"

"Oh yes. I saved you a copy of the paper." He pulled a folded newspaper from behind him and handed it to his son. The paper was folded right to it. Joe stood there and read the article, Dusty at his side.

"Hey boy. This is all about you. Hmm, I don't care much for that 'mongrel' part, and the numbers aren't quite right, but this is great. I'll thank Florence. I'll keep this forever."

"Well, there was another article that she didn't give them, written by a reporter. It said you were a group of four, not five, but I didn't manage to get a copy of it. Son, we're all quite proud of you, and Dusty too, of course."

Dog Saves Four on Patrol When Mine Explodes

Mascot Who Set Off Land Charge Now On Way Home With Pontiac Man

A returning troop ship is expected soon to bring to this country a "veteran" who holds a high place among four members of the 20th antiaircraft battery.

He is "Dusty," a four year old mongrel Australian dog. He is credited with saving the lives of four men while on patrol duty when he set off a land mine just ahead of the men.

DEWEY

Owner of the dog is Sgt. Wilbur J. Dewey, technician fourth grade of 27 Clark street, Pontiac. One of the men who was on patrol is Corp. Robert Woods, technician fifth grade of the Cadillac apartments.

"Dusty" was trotting 15 feet ahead of the four men along a mountain trail in northern Luzon.

Suddenly there was an explosion. The dog crumpled to the ground. The four men were knocked down by the concussion.

"Dusty" had tripped off a land mine ahead of the patrol. But miraculously, he lived. The men cared for his wounds, including a broken leg. They've healed and "Dusty" has earned his trip to his new home in full measure.

Sgt. Dewey was in service when war was declared and shortly after was sent to Australia. He found "Dusty" there about three years ago. The five men have agreed jointly to look after "Dusty's" future and Sgt. Dewey will establish a home for him.

Dewey's parents are Mr. and Mrs. Stuart J. Dewey of the Clark street address.

Joe called this was his army suit picture.

Joe spent two nights with his folks, then headed for Kentucky. It was all he could do to put it off even two nights, but they were his family. *That was great, seeing Serena and her husband again. I like Mort. It was fun seeing those old friends. Dad doesn't look so good. Life seems to be wearing him down.*

I think working in the shop and running the farm is too much for him. He still drinks an awful lot too.

* * *

He drove away from Stuart and Mildred's house at five in the morning. He was used to early hours, and he had a lot of road to cover. It seemed like the roads went through every small town in the state, and nothing was highway. He spent fifteen hours thinking the same thoughts over and over.

This drive to Kentucky seems way too long.

A hundred small towns to drive through and here's another one.

I wonder if Hazel quit that job she had.

I wonder what her dad is really like. She says he's a big man.

Not a letter since I left Australia. Maybe she quit writing me.

Does she really think I'm coming to Kentucky?

Maybe she doesn't want me to, and this was just a game. What do coal miners talk about?

This drive to Kentucky seems way too long.

Then his busy mind started over at the top of his short list of questions and concerns.

He finally got to Graham—at least that's where he thought he was. *Man, this's the same size as every other tiny town I just drove through that had just one stop sign, a gas station and a bar. These streets are more like country roads than city streets. Geez, I have no idea which way to go. No signs, dirt roads. I'm going to have to stop for directions. I'll pull in that fruit and vegetable stand on the side of the road.*

He got out and walked over to the woman who must have been the farmer's wife that grew the produce. "Hello, Ma'am."

"Hello yourself, young fella. What can I do for you? You're not from around here."

"You noticed, huh? How, exactly—my accent?"

"Well, that too, I suppose, but I knew before you said a word. I'd recognize anybody who lives within ten miles of Graham."

"Oh. Do you know the Stewarts, by any chance?"

"Eli and Lela's bunch? Sure. Most of their brood have married and moved on though. Just Hazel is...say, you must be Joe—Joe Dewey. Is that Dusty in your car?"

He was startled to be recognized. "Um, yes, that's him. You want to meet him?"

"I shore do! He's a celebrity around here. He saved your life, I understand."

"Yes, Ma'am. He did." Joe whistled and Dusty sprang through the open window of the car and trotted over and sat by him. "This is Dusty." She dropped to one knee and gave the dog a big hug.

"Everybody's gonna be jealous I seen y'all first. You ain't been to Hazel's yet?"

"No. In fact, I'm having some trouble with the directions."

Just then a car drove by, honked and waved, and Dusty tore out after it. "Dusty, no! Get back here!"

"He do that much?"

"He's been chasing Jeeps and cars since we've been together." Dusty trotted back and sat by Joe. "The directions?"

"Oh sure, it's easy to get there from here." She gave him a coy smile. "Some places you cain't get to from here, but theirs is easy." She pointed down the road. "Yonder's a little ol' bridge, and you cross it. If'n you look to the right you can see her house across Copper's Ditch and up the hill. They's five houses and theirs is the first on the hill. Stay on the road and git on the road on the other side what don't exactly connect, but you'll see it. Ya cain't miss it." She gave the startled soldier a big hug, then tousled the hair on Dusty's head.

"I cain't believe I met you first. Joe, the whole county is lookin' fer you. Li'l Hazel's been talking you up for a long time now. You git going, don't keep her waitin'." She shooed him off like a swarm of flies.

"Thank you, Ma'am. What was your name?"

"Debbie Jo. Haz will know who I am. Go on now. She'll be there. There ain't never nobody not home there."

He tipped his hat and opened the door for Dusty. They settled in for a brief ride. *I guess there's no limit to how many negatives you can cram in a sentence. I think she meant there's always someone home. Who knows?*

Her directions don't make any sense at all. Yonder—where the hell is that? And two roads that don't exactly connect, and I'm to get on the second one from the first? Geeza Lou, this is a different world.

While the directions sounded odd, they got him there in ten minutes. He stopped at the little bridge and stared to the right, and sure enough there was a hill with five houses lined up. He had a target. He crossed the bridge, drove till he could cut over to the road parallel to the road he was on, then turned back toward the hill. He slowed down at "Copper's Ditch" and took a close look. It was copper colored with rocks turning orange from the stain of the water. *Now I understand the name.*

Joe pulled in the dirt drive at the first house up the hill and stepped out of his 1938 Chevy. *Good car. Lots of miles on it, but it ran good and got me here.* He stretched the kinks out of his back as he looked around. He saw Hazel bounding off the porch heading for him. He'd have known her anywhere from the pictures she sent him. Then he saw her daddy; a hulking man built for the long, hard hours working deep underground in the coal mines. He was coming at him too. Hazel saw this and slowed to a walk, then stopped. Clearly she was letting her daddy get to Joe first.

Joe stepped up to the big man and extended his hand. Joe was an average size guy at five-feet-eight-inches and about a hundred and sixty pounds, but his hand was lost in the grip of this man. "I'm Eli Stewart, Hazel's pappy. She's comin' right behind me."

It was a challenge for just a moment, as Eli squeezed hard. Joe had a sense that this man could crush his hand if he chose to, so he squeezed back as hard as he could. They held for a minute until Eli saw the grimace in Joe's eyes. He let go and grinned. "Nice grip, boy. Kinda small hands, though. The trick to never getting' your hand crushed is to grip the other guy high on his hand before he gets a grip; like this. Teach that to your own boys someday." He demonstrated.

"I will."

There was no shy staring at each other when Hazel got to Joe—she'd broken into a run. There weren't any silly questions and statements. There was just a big hug as Hazel ran past her daddy and leaped into Joe's arms. There also wasn't much lingering in their first kiss with Eli so close. "Okay, you've said your hellos. C'mon to the house with me and meet Lela."

As Eli led them past the hand pump they used for water in the house, he looked at Dusty. "Your dog sure stays close to you."

"Always, sir."

Eli opened the door and walked in to his partner in life, tiny Lelia Stewart—Lela for short. She was all of ninety pounds and four-foot-ten to Eli's three hundred plus at about six-foot-two. He put his massive arm around his little wife. "This here's Lela, Hazel's momma." He smiled down at his tiny wife. "She's one tough woman. You know, she birthed a baby every two years for a long while, then waited three years and had our twins, Elma and Velma, then four years for JC, and then four more years for our last baby, Li'l Hazel. She had my babies for well over twenty years."

Eli and Lelia Stewart

Joe learned immediately that Lela's small form belied her spirit. She stepped up close, took his hand in her little ones, and fixed him with her stare. "Good to meet you, young fella. Just where you stayin' while you're visiting Little Hazel. You cain't stay here."

Joe leaned back just a bit, afraid to take a step away from this woman and let go of her hand. Hazel was all smiles and promises, Eli was a hulking menace, but oddly enough tiny Lela was the one who made him flinch.

He was captivated by this woman with skin like leather and curly salt and pepper hair down to her shoulders. "Don't know yet, Ma'am. I thought I'd find a place today. I've got some money from the service."

"Ain't no hotels about. Nary much in the way of restaurants neither." Lela kept him caught in her stare. "I think Big Hazel and Phutney will keep you for a time, and you'll eat here with us. After that we'll have to wait'n see."

"Uh, Big Hazel and who?"

"Phutney. He's our boy and Big Hazel's his wife. Eli, show him over to their place."

They walked out the back door again, past the pump toward his car. "Where do Phutney and Big Hazel live?"

Eli lifted his big hand and pointed to the only house within five hundred feet. It was a small house about twenty feet away. Joe had assumed it was an outbuilding of theirs. "There. Just behind them is another of our boys, Felt, and his wife, Willie Curtis. Go on now. Li'l Hazel will introduce you and get you settled. I'll fetch your case and put it on their steps."

Hazel took his hand and pulled Joe toward the house next door.

Joe spoke quietly. "Little Hazel? Big Hazel? How big is she?"

Hazel just laughed and squeezed his hand tighter. "You'll see. She cain't walk through that door. She's so big she has to stay in the house all the time."

She burst into the house with Joe in tow. Dusty bounded in with them. A solid woman, clearly older than Hazel, was ironing. She looked up, set the iron down and smiled. "You must be Joe. Welcome." She gave him a strong handshake. "I hope this is your dog." Dusty was on his hind legs licking Big Hazel. "Sure is a friendly thing."

"I'm sorry. Should I not have let him in?"

"Well, Phutney don't take to dogs in the house, but this one can be the exception. Dusty, right?"

"Yes ma'am. He saved my life."

"We all heard all about that. Hazel's been keeping us up on all the goin's on in Australia with you and Dusty. This here dog is as famous in these parts as Therman's mule."

"Uh, pardon me?"

"Never mind. You'll hear him bray now and again. It's like nails on a chalkboard."

"I see. And you're, uh, Big Hazel?"

She laughed—a deep, infectious laugh. "First off, why are you staring at me like that? Did Li'l Hazel tell you some nonsense about me being too big to fit through the door?"

"Um, well, um..."

"Never mind, Joe. Hazel, you little devil. What were you thinkin' telling that to Joe? Well, I'm certainly bigger than that little thing you're in love with. But I'm older than her, and married, and big and little is just an easy way to know who people are talking about. James will be in later. You can eat with us tonight."

"Oh, Momma said he should stay with you guys while he's here and to tell you to come over and eat with us. I think everybody's comin' to dinner who can get here. Sorry. I forgot. I should've told you yesterday."

"No problem, Hazel. James and me wouldn't miss it for anything."

"Excuse me. Who is James?"

"Phutney. I call him by his given name. Nobody else does."

"Well, Lela said I'd be eating with them and staying with you."

"Well, okay then. If that's what Ms. Stewart said, that's what you'll do. Sit down and I'll make some coffee." She watched as Little Hazel and Joe pulled out chairs from the kitchen table and sat down. "So you're gonna call Ms. Stewart, 'Lela'?" She put a hard "s" on "Ms" like it was a "z."

Joe was nervous and looked at his honey. "I don't know. That's how Eli introduced her. What should I call her?"

Big Hazel ignored her little sister-in-law's efforts to get into the conversation. "Let's start with her daddy. I wouldn't recommend calling him Eli."

"What then?"

"Well, I been married to Phutney for fifteen years, and his daddy is Mr. Stewart, and his momma is Ms. Stewart. I guess you could call him, 'Sir' or some-such. It's up to you, of course, but his sons-in-law and daughters-in-law don't much call him daddy or Eli. Same thing goes for Ms. Stewart. I expect he'll straighten you out if he don't like what you choose."

Joe kept sneaking looks at Hazel, which wasn't surprising. What was surprising though was that he was watching her lift her coffee cup and set it back down. Every time she reached for it he smiled. He answered Big Hazel in a distracted sort of way. "Okay then, that sounds safe. Mr. and Ms. Stewart it is."

"Joe, why do you keep looking at my coffee cup?"

"Dearest Hazel, you are lefthanded!"

"Sure. So?"

"I've had nothing but trouble because I'm a lefty. I can't believe my girl is a lefty too."

Big Hazel inserted herself into the conversation. "Nobody around here cares, but you should see the way she puts paper turned all the way around to write anything. It's funny looking."

"Me too. All our letters to each other have been written with our left hands. Wow."

"I suppose."

"That's great. Our kids will probably be lefthanded too, I guess."

"I don't know about that. Mama and Daddy aren't, but I am. It can go either way."

"I suppose. Lefthanded! How about that?" Years later they found it funny that neither of their children were lefthanded.

"Okay you two. Joe, bring your stuff on in, and you can stay in James Truman's room. Him and Shirley Dean can sleep on opposite ends of the couch for a while. The outhouse is across the road. Watch out for snakes. Toilet paper is on the cabinet by the stove. Go on now, get your stuff." She gave Joe a little shove to get the young couple going. Dusty followed close behind them.

Joe tripped over his suitcase. Eli had left it on the steps, just as he said he would. "Let's go get my other stuff from the car."

Hazel was all chatty as they walked to his car. "Most of the family is comin' to dinner tonight to meet you. We'll have quite a crowd. Gene, my oldest brother, he's the toughest man in Muhlenberg County, well, next to Daddy. He wears a pistol, just like out west. His wife Irene is really nice. Don't know why she married Gene. Then Earl and Martha will be here, Earl looks like a movie star. And Elma, but Bennie won't come, and Velma and Henry Earl, she wouldn't miss it—she'll be my maid of honor when we get married, and Nellie and John, and Archie and Willie 'cause they live right here, and JC and Lena. Umm, I think that's all who's comin' tonight. Of course, Hazel and Phutney will be here. Oh, and my sister Mae and her husband will be here, cause they live just across that field. The others are futher away, and it would take 'em too long just for dinner."

Joe smiled at his darling. "Honey, you know there's an 'r' in further."

Hazel laughed. "Maybe up in Michigan, but hereabouts it's pronounced, 'fuuther'. It's like, well, how would you say the name of a cow's milk sack?"

"You mean an udder?"

"Yes. So it's udder nonsense to put two 'r's in futher." She laughed at her rhyme.

"You mean utter, not udder, Honey."

"You're not makin' any sense now, Baby. Them's the same words."

"Okay, fine. Forgive me if I forget and add an 'r' when I say it. Well, I guess that's enough people for me to meet in one day. At least I know their names from your letters, but putting all those faces and names together will be tough in one night."

She took his arm as he lifted his smaller bag from the car and beamed up at him. "You'll do great!"

* * *

"Dinner time, Joe!" Hazel called it out as she burst into Big Hazel and Phutney's house. He was ready and took her hand as they walked across the yard to her folks' house. Dusty followed a few steps behind Hazel, with Phutney and Big Hazel just behind him. Several cars and some buggies were there. People were still going in and some were just standing around outside. A group of men stood near the well; one waved them over. As they neared, Gene, Eli's oldest boy, waved Hazel off. "We just want to meet Joe, baby doll. You go on in. We'll be along shortly."

She gave Joe's hand a squeeze and ran off to the house. Joe, Dusty still trailing close behind, walked over to the group with Phutney. "I'm Gene, this is Earl, Henry, Archie, John, and the short guy is JC. 'Course you know Phutney. We just wanted to have a quick visit before dinner."

"Well, here I am. I don't think we have much time, so a quick visit about what?"

"Well, Hazel is our baby sister, though Henry and John just married into the family, but they's kin right enough. We won't put up with Hazel being hurt. She's waited a long time for the right man. She'd barely even go out with the young men around here in Muhlenberg County, waitin' for the right guy to come along. She should've married four or five years ago, but here we are. You think you're that man?"

"She thinks so, and so do I."

Gene pulled back his jacket to show his revolver. "You may've made it through the war, but that don't mean you'll make it out of Kentucky if our baby sister gets hurt."

"You gonna fight me, all of you, or just shoot me? For all of Hazel being an angel, you folks aren't the friendliest I've run across."

"Oh now, Joe, Gene's just talking. We don't..."

"Shut up Henry Earl. You just married into the family when you married Velma. You got no say here right now."

"Wait just a minute Gene. We want Joe to know how much we love Little Hazel, but c'mon now."

"You shut up too John. I thought we agreed on this."

Joe had been quietly rolling up his sleeves as they had their disagreement. His muscles rippled as his rich, quiet voice addressed the group of men. At just five feet eight inches, Joe was not the tallest man in the group. He knew he had to establish his position now, right up front.

Dusty sensed the tension, and sat at his master's feet, growling with his impressive fangs bared. The short white hair on the back of his neck was standing straight up. His oddly pointed ears seemed to be almost twitching.

"Boys, if you're going to do something, do it now. In ten minutes, I'm going into dinner, and I'll not be keeping Hazel waiting. I'll say this one time; showing up this week doesn't mean I haven't loved her for almost three years. If we're gonna fight, I figure Dusty can take out two of you, and I'll have to manage the rest; that's assuming you fight fair and don't use knives or that gun. I'm a boxer, but I can fight dirty too, and I don't even *want* to remember what all I did in the war. I didn't come to fight. I just want to meet Hazel's family and have dinner."

Gene looked down at the snarling dog for a minute, then at Joe. "This here's the dog that saved your life?" Joe nodded. "Well now, nobody wants to fight. We just want you to know how we feel. Looks like you're gonna be family."

Henry Earl stepped up and inserted himself between Gene and Joe, grabbed Joe's hand and pumped it fast. He wore a grin from ear to ear. "Let's eat. Ms. Stewart don't like to call us twice." The tension evaporated. Several men laughed and they all started toward the house. Henry was close to Joe and spoke in a whisper. "Good job. I was a little worried."

Joe whispered back to him. "I think I was closer to being dead just now than at any time during the war."

As they walked inside, Hazel showed Joe where to sit at the big table and moved her chair over so their legs touched. "What was that all about?"

"Nothing. They were just taking my measure."

"What's that mean?"

"Nothing. Hush, Honey. Eli wants to start."

Several were milling about in the dining area, trying to figure out seats. There were more bodies than chairs. Eli stepped up to Gene. "Leave that gun in the drawer over there. I won't have it at my table."

"I don't see why not, Daddy. I'll..." Eli moved fast for a big man. He backhanded his oldest boy and knocked him across the room through a knot of three other men.

"What'd I say, Gene?"

"Ye'sir." Gene levered himself up off the floor and grumbled as he unbuckled his holster and put it and his sidearm in the drawer.

Eli surveyed the crowd and locked his eyes on Joe. "Joe, everybody ought to meet Dusty too. Bring him on in. He don't take too much space, and his manners are better than some of my boys." Eli laughed loudly at this own joke, which startled everyone. Joe popped the door open and Dusty slipped through the crowded room to find Hazel and pushed up close.

Henry Earl found that amusing. "Is Dusty your dog, Joe, or Hazels?

Joe looked down at his trusty side-kick and sighed. "I guess he's making a transition of some kind. I think that's good."

"Maybe he's accepting her as part of your family already."

"I believe he is, Henry." They both looked at Dusty and Hazel. She was cradling his big head and planting a smooch between his pointed ears.

Felt nodded. "Movin' into a family ought to be easy."

Somehow the voice of tiny Lela cut through the din. "Sit down, all a' ya. The foods hot." Everybody quickly found a seat till the chairs were full, then a couple of men pulled up wooden boxes from the next room. They were finally all seated but still very loud. The little woman surveyed her rowdy family from the wood stove. "Quiet 'em down, Eli."

"**All right! Quiet y'all!** Be still. Good. Lela?"

She nodded. "Henry Earl, you pray."

Joe gave Hazel's hand a squeeze as he let out a sigh. He wasn't a praying man, but he gave a silent prayer too. *God get me through this dinner.*

* * *

Joe was figuring out how to proceed as he sat with Phutney at their table the next morning. Big Hazel poured coffee for the two men in simple, plain cups on saucers. "Mr. Stewart wants me to get a job and live here for a while before he'll agree for Hazel to marry me. I guess that's fair. He wants to get to know me."

Big Hazel spoke up from the stove. "They weren't so fussy when they were trying to get the other ten married and out of the house. Haz is the baby, so that makes it different, I guess."

"Hell, they didn't care who I married so long as I moved out." Phutney laughed. "Then I built this place in their yard. I didn't go too far." He poured coffee from his cup into the saucer, lifted it to his lips and loudly slurped it in.

"Interesting way to drink coffee, Phutney."

Phutney took another loud slurp from his saucer. "The cup is to get the coffee to you without spillin' it. The saucer is to let it cool quick and drink it. Try it, Joe."

"No thanks. I'll take your word for it, but I'll use the cup."

"Suit yourself. I hear Pepsi Cola's hiring. All you got to do is drive the truck and deliver the cases of soda."

"That'd be okay. I could try it."

"Sure thing. Drive over to Henderson and apply. They're selling so much soda they can't get it delivered everywhere. At five cents a bottle I'm surprised anybody can afford to buy it. Henry Earl, now he loves Dr. Pepper. Drinks eight or more a day. Nasty stuff. I'd say he skips meals so they can afford it, but then when you take a good look at Henry, you gotta figure I'm wrong. He don't miss too many meals."

"Henry's a coal miner, too?"

"Everybody is unless they own a store or something. It's the only business around. But the mines are having trouble. Peabody's strip-mining Muhlenberg County and turning everything upside down."

"Turning things upside down? What's that mean?"

"Just what I said. They take these giant steam shovels, rip up hunks of ground bigger'n a house, lift it up and dump it upside down. Then the coal is close to the surface and easy to get at. No more underground mining—at least not deep underground—and *not* here. The deep coal will just stay in the ground.

"It'll put everybody out of work. This here will be a ghost town in a few years. My hours have already been cut, so I take whatever jobs I can get to stay afloat."

"Me and Hazel are going to move to Michigan so I can get a job in the factory, building cars. You could too."

Phutney looked over at Big Hazel and smiled. "Nope. This is home, and we'll die right here someday. Cain't say it's wrong for you to move north. It'd be good for Li'l Hazel to get out of here. Two of mom's sisters married and moved to Michigan years ago. It works for some."

"Well, tomorrow I'll go over to Henderson and check out that job. Anything will be okay so long as it pays what I need while I'm here."

The next day Joe, Hazel and Dusty took his car to Henderson. Joe found the Pepsi office. It was pretty obvious with the giant, neon bottle of soda on their roof.

Hazel, why don't you and Dusty go down to that place there and get something to drink? They've got outdoor tables, I see. I'll join you when I'm done."

"Okay Joe. C'mon, Dusty."

The two walked down the street, admiring what little was in the store windows. There were only two other people sitting at the outdoor tables, so Hazel sat at an empty table and Dusty sat on his haunches next to her.

"Yes, Miss. What'll you have?"

"Well, Sir, I believe I'll have a nice, icy cold Pepsi. My friend here," and she glanced at Dusty, "will just sit with me." She made a pretentious arm movement like they were all in a movie, and the young server laughed.

"Right away. I'll just be a minute.'

After the young man left, another young customer came and sat down across from her. "I'm sorry, but this table's taken."

"I know. I'm takin' half, and you're takin' the other half." He laughed like it was quite funny. "I'm Fisher. And you are?"

"I am asking you again to leave me alone."

He skootched his chair close to her. "Oh c'mon, you can be friendlier than that." He reached out and took her hand in his. She pulled away, but he held her in his grip.

"I think you should let go, Fisher." She glanced around and noticed the couple at the other table quickly walking away.

"Why is that? I'm having fun."

She turned and tried to get up but he prevented her from moving enough. She raised her voice and struggled and that did it. Suddenly the man screamed as Dusty came up between his legs, growling, and clamped his teeth on something tender. Fisher shrieked like he was dying. Dusty shook his head like he did when he caught a rabbit, banging his big head back and forth on the man's thighs. Fisher threw his hands into the air and screamed for help.

"Dusty, let him go." Dusty moved back and stood next to Hazel, his growl deepened, fangs still exposed.

Fisher stood up and she could see his pants were ripped and the zipper was nearly torn off. He grabbed his crotch and ran like a demon was chasing him. Just as he was turning the corner, Joe arrived. "What was that all about?"

"Dusty did *not* like the way that young man was behaving."

"Oh, now what did you do, Dusty?"

"Joe, he protected me. That guy grabbed me and wouldn't let go. That is, until Dusty sank his teeth into his, well, let's just say the boy ran away so fast that maybe he can still be a daddy someday." She giggled.

Joe hitched his trousers up slightly. "I've seen Dusty...well, never mind. The kid will be okay, you think?"

"He seemed way more scared than hurt, although he looked silly holding himself like that as he ran. But Dusty taught him a good lesson." She hugged Dusty's head. "Good boy, and thank you for being my protector."

"Well, I got the job. Pepsi thinks I have potential."

* * *

This Pepsi job is plenty boring, but the check each week makes it worth it. Eli will see I can take care of Hazel. And my pay wasn't this regular overseas—lots of glitches in the system. Okay, this load goes to Central City. No problem. An easy drive with lots of hills.

The hill was gradual going up, and the Pepsi truck, a giant bottle of soda painted bright and proud on both sides, struggled a bit climbing the incline. The truck was going forty-five miles an hour when it topped the hill and picked up speed before Joe could stop it. *What the hell is that giant tractor doing? I can't stop this thing!*

Joe had to make an instant decision. He could either smash into the tractor and maybe get hurt or killed, or he could dodge it. It was a tough decision made worse by the four-foot-deep ditches on both sides of the road. He swerved into the steep ditch on the right. The top-heavy truck pitched over on its side like a playful whale breaching the surface and splashing back down. The din of hundreds of bottles smashing together combined with the noise of the truck trying to plow its side through the ground. It came to a sudden stop, nearly wrenching Joe's arms out of their sockets as he hung on to the steering wheel. The silence that followed was disturbing. No birds, no crickets, no nothing. Silence.

Joe got out and shook his head, checking himself for injuries.

Man, I'm glad Dusty stayed with Hazel today. And just what am I going to tell her? Oh man, and her dad.

He looked over the truck and knew it was a goner. Except for one wheel still spinning, it sure seemed dead.

The farmer driving the tractor heard the crash behind him and stopped his rig. He ran back to see it. "Hey young fella! You okay?"

Joe's hearing was coming back. "I guess so. I didn't see you there. You were going awful slow over the crest of that hill."

"Nope, you shore didn't." The farmer took off his cap like a funeral was passing him as he looked at the remains of the truck, with its proud, bright Pepsi picture now facing straight up at the sky.

"Think I ought to shoot it?"

The farmer laughed. "Nah, it's just a truck, not a horse. 'Sides, it's done keeled over. It's already dead. Need a ride?"

"Guess so. I'll call 'em to tell them about their truck. I guess I need another job."

The old farmer turned to stare at the wreck again. "Yep, I reckon so. Climb up and I'll take you where I'm going. From there you're on your own. They's a phone there, though. You get settled on the back end, right there, and I'll be just a minute." It took a bit to get settled in and feel secure enough that he wouldn't fall off the tractor. By then the farmer was back with a bottle of Pepsi in each of his overall's six pockets.

The ride to the phone was slow, loud, and dusty for the devastated young veteran. Joe watched the world crawl by through a thick cloud of dust as the tractor steadily plodded along the dirt road. *What will I do next? Be a coal miner? As much as I don't want to work underground, I wish they were hiring more than firing people at the mines.*

*　*　*

Hazel was unperturbed by Joe's sudden unemployment. "Let's wait a couple of days, then we can go see Skeeter and Lena. He always cheers me up."

"Skeeter?"

"You know, my baby brother. He's next to me in age."

"Why's he called, 'Skeeter'?"

"I dunno, he just is."

"What's his real name?"

"JC. I told you that. He got home from the war over a year ago, and now they're building a house. I'd love to see it."

"What's JC stand for?"

"Just JC. That's his name."

Joe sighed. "We can go anytime you want. I guess I've got the time now."

"I talked to the guy at the telegraph office about a job today. Thought I might get it too. But he got fresh with me, and I slapped him."

"What did he say to you? Or did he touch you?"

"Well, he came out of his little office and talked like we were real close, you know. Then he tried to take my hand."

"What did you do?"

"I didn't hafta do much. I jerked my hand away and Dusty almost took a chunk out of his leg. He ran back in that little office right quick, too."

"You want me to go see him and make him apologize?"

"No, silly. Dusty took care of it."

Hazel squeezed his leg with her hand. "Stop the car and pull off the road."

"Why?"

"No reason we have to get back from the store so fast. Nobody around. Let's just, you know."

Joe pulled the car over to the side of the road, turned off the ignition and pulled his lady close. Just before their lips met she pulled her face back. "Hey, did you keep any Pepsi from your truck?"

His laughter put the kiss off a few seconds. "No. C'mere you."

* * *

That night Eli talked to Joe about helping him with a grape arbor. "I need some help moving the timber for it. It's just down the hill. We can probably move it quick tomorrow morning after breakfast. The mines are shut down this week."

"Sure, Mr. Stewart, I'll be here and ready. What kind of wood you using?"

"Railroad ties. You ever move any, Joe?"

"I don't think so. Where do you buy those?"

"You don't. They're just lyin' about for people to use. I've done it lots of times.

"The railroad doesn't care if you take them? Seems like they'd have them piled up in places to use."

"And that's what we're gonna do, son. We're gonna use 'em. I don't suppose they care—leastwise they've never come up here to talk with me about it. First thing tomorrow."

"Yes sir. Night."

* * *

The next morning Eli and Joe ate, as usual, with whoever showed up at Lela's table. Today was quiet with just the two of them and Lela, fussing at her wood-burning stove. It was a normal breakfast of biscuits and gravy, along with some kind of meat. Little bitty legs and backs fried in the gravy. Joe took a piece with the biscuits and gravy.

"This isn't a small chicken, is it?"

Eli didn't look up from his plate as he ate. "Nope—ain't nothin' like a chicken."

Joe didn't ask any more questions about it, and Eli didn't offer any more information about the mystery meat. He also didn't waste any time lingering. "C'mon Joe. Every man to an axe, every axe to a tree—let's hit it."

The hill wasn't that steep, or even that long, but it was hot and humid out already, and they were planning on carrying these things up the hill by hand. *Well, I suppose two of us carrying one at a time won't be too tough, whatever they weigh. Eli's a big guy.*

The pile of ties was fairly big. They were all treated with creosol, and when Joe picked up the end of one, he grunted and dropped it. "Way heavier than I thought. Maybe we should borrow a truck."

Eli turned and just stared at him like he'd just cursed his mother. "Why would we do that? I guess we might strap one at a time to the Model A, but that's more work than it's worth. Just pick it up and let's get going. Oh, and keep your shirt on. That creosol will eat your skin off."

"You have any gloves?"

"Nope."

"Well, I'm glad I don't have skin on my hands, then."

"You gonna complain all day or work?" Eli turned away to look over another railroad tie.

Joe picked up one end of the tie he'd just dropped and waited for Eli to get the other end while he gauged the length of the tie—it looked to be about eight and a half feet long. He looked up and watched in awe as Eli slung one tie onto his shoulder. "Joe, hoist that one there onto my other shoulder, quick like, cause they're heavy."

Trying to not let his eyes betray him, Joe grunted and wrestled the tie onto Eli's shoulder. Eli started walking immediately. "Pick up yours and let's go. We'll have to make several trips down here."

Joe watched the huge man, his future father-in-law, start up the hill with two massive railroad ties on his shoulders, looked down at the pile of them and sighed. *Damn. Here we go.* He wrestled a tie onto one shoulder and staggered. *No way can I carry two of these. Eli's crazy, but man, he's strong. Now **this** is a story I'll tell my kids someday.*

He lurched up the hill, stopping to take breaks to breathe on the way. When he finally got to the house, Eli was leaning on the well, waiting for him. "Thought you might have changed your mind about movin' 'em. You took your good ol' time comin' up 'at hill."

Joe shrugged the heavy beam off his shoulder and sat on the grass. "I'm fine; just need to breathe for a bit."

Eli started laughing. "Sorry Joe," he choked out as he tried to stop. "You done good. I'd a thought you might not get up here with it. I'm not sure anybody hereabouts carries them alone but me—and now you. Take your time. I know this is tough work. We could walk up the road if you like, 'cause it's not as steep as the yard is, but it's a lot futher to carry 'em."

Joe sighed. *I suppose it wouldn't be prudent to tell Eli there's an 'r' in further.* "No, no, let's take the hill and keep it shorter."

They made three more trips, with Eli carrying two ties the next two trips and just one on the last one. Joe took one each time, and his rest breaks got longer. They finally threw the last two down.

"Thanks, Joe. I'm getting' old. That woulda took a lot longer without your help. When you want to put the arbor together? Of course, we've got to dig post holes first."

"Many rocks in this soil?" Joe grew up on a farm and knew all about digging rocks out of fields.

"Some, but not bad. See the rock circle around the well there?"

"Yeah. That's about four feet tall. That's a lot of rocks."

"We built it out of the rocks we got out of the hole when we dug the well. That's how many there are here."

Damn, that's a lot of rocks. "Mr. Stewart, we can dig them today if you want. I don't think I'll be up for building the arbor today, though."

"Good enough. Let me get the shovels." He walked back twenty minutes later with two spade shovels. "This is what I got. Here's yours."

"Without post-hole diggers these holes are going to be a lot bigger than they need to be."

"I'm a big guy, and I want the arbor to stand for a long, long time. The bigger the holes, the more rock and cement we'll dump in, and the stronger she'll be. Besides, they'll have to be big holes to get the rocks out of them."

Eli leaned on the shovel for a minute and just looked at the pile of railroad ties. "I'll tell you how strong these here ties are. My boy Phutney got tired of fixing his mailbox every time the idiot up the hill there drove home drunk and knocked it over. That guy did it twice a month, drunk as a skunk. He'd knock it down, Phutney would stick another post in the ground and nail the box on it. After a few months of that, Phutney dug himself a really big hole, put one of these ties in place and filled it all in with cement. He poured in bag after bag along with more buckets of gravel than I could count. The next time that id-jit up there came flying by in his car, he slammed into it head on."

Joe looked over at Phutney's mailbox. Sure enough, it was on a railroad tie, with most of the tie in the ground. "What happened?"

Eli turned to look at the mailbox. "Well, the post and the box are still there, but the boy wrecked his car and got thow'd out. Broke both his legs."

"That's awful."

"Why? He's the one what hit the post. It was the same place it's always been. He was dumb enough to think he could just keep doing it and nothin' would ever change. Something did change, and it worked too. It fixed his aim."

"Sir?"

"He didn't never hit it again after he broke his legs."

"Phutney didn't get in trouble?"

"Well, shore he did, at least a little. He had to answer to the judge for breaking the boy's legs, but the judge knew that stupid boy from bein' in his courtroom lots of times—drunk and disturbin' the peace, you know. He did what was right. He warned Phutney not to fix his mailbox up so bad it would kill the boy, then he let him go. Long enough break? We should get to diggin'."

A couple of hours into the digging, Joe was drinking from an ice-cold jug of water from the pump and watching Dusty sleep. "Why don't you dig for a while, Dusty? You're pretty good at it." The dog languidly lifted his head, licked his nose, and lowered his head again to return to his interrupted nap. *Of course, you're from Australia, and you know better than to work hard in this heat and humidity. We could learn from you, buddy.*

The arbor became a three-day project, but finally, there it stood. "One of my boys is making a porch swing like on my side porch. We can hang that from it when he gets it finished. For now, I just want the grapevines in the ground."

* * *

Hazel came out and watched the arbor project for hours at a time, then drifted off to do other things when she got bored. Dusty must have been bored with the project too because he usually went with her. The day it was finished she started in on Joe about going to see Skeeter and Lena.

"Honey, I've got a lead on a gas station near Madisonville. They closed it but I might get to open it up and run it again. If I can make it work, that'd really be something."

"Gasoline stinks. But daddy would like you havin' another job. Okay, you check that out and we'll go to Skeeter's next week."

The company was glad to have someone try to make the station work. They offered Joe the manager position, since there was only him to work there. The company office gave Joe a uniform and a company cigarette lighter. He opened the station right away. That weekend they planned on going to Skeeter and Lena's.

Hazel's brother, JC, aka Skeeter, was the tenth youngest of her family. She was the only one younger than him—there were four years between them. That was the largest gap between any of the eleven children of Eli and Lela. She liked Lena, and Joe thought he'd like them both based on what Hazel said about them and what little he knew from his big dinner with the family.

Their young boys were in the yard when they pulled up, looking like tiny farmers with their hands holding the straps on their little denim overalls. They were laughing as they watched the chicken pen. The hens were running around like they were chasing each other. Hazel knew what they were doing. She used to do it too. "Whatcha doing, guys?"

The youngest held up a tiny jelly jar. "We caught some gashoppers."

His brother chimed in, not wanting to be left out. "We pull their back legs off, the hoppin' ones, and toss 'em in the pen. The chickens go crazy chasin' 'em. The grasshoppers never, ever get away."

His little brother solemnly took off his little cap and held it with his head down like he'd seen his daddy do when funeral coaches drove slowly past. "Poor ol' gashoppers."

Joe laughed at the boys. "Let's hope nobody tears your legs off and leaves you for the bears."

"We got no bears around here."

Joe just smiled. "I think you missed the point. Have fun."

They went inside where Lena had some coffee waiting for them on the stove. The men each took a cup and sat in the living room while Hazel and Lena talked in the kitchen.

Joe looked around at the unfinished house. It was livable, but the paneling wasn't all on the walls yet, and it seemed too short. "You're doing a fine job on the house. Say, this isn't an eight-foot ceiling, is it?"

"No. We're not that tall and everything was cheaper if we went with a seven-foot ceiling. It'll work for us."

"So, what do you do for a living, JC?"

"Well, Joe, I work in a slaughterhouse, and my job changes every week. Some weeks I dress out the animals we kill, and some weeks I'm the guy what kills 'em."

"Steers, or what?"

"Oh sure, beef cattle. People even sell the factory their old cows that run dry. We do sheep and pigs too, but nothin' small as a chicken."

"So, when you get the job of putting them down, say a steer, how do you go about that?"

"You know, we get people every week who tour the place. I guess out of curiosity or just wanting to see how we kill animals—city folk, not hunters and farmers. They all do their own share of killing. The city folk, now they find it either really different from anything they know or just plain awful. That's why they come.

"Okay, we move the steer into a tall trough it can't move around in, and I use a sledgehammer to knock it in the head. They usually go down on the first hit, but some of them just won't die easy. After they're down we cut their throats and they bleed out. After that we meat-hook 'em and the carcass is pulled to the next crew to get gutted, skinned and hung."

As Joe thought about that, JC started laughing hard.

"Nothing you said sounds funny."

"No, but I can still see one prim old lady, just after I'd hammered a steer, insisting to her son that she was fine, and she was gonna stay to see what I did next. But when I slit that cow's throat, the old gal threw up so hard she almost passed out. They carried her out. See, I think that was funny."

"I suppose. Grisly work, huh?"

"Guess so. You get so used to it you don't notice much. It's a job. I'm not squeamish about it. Neither is Lena. That hamburger she's frying up was a cow once too."

"You do any deer?"

"Not at the plant, but most of us dress 'em out now and again for folks who know us. You deer hunt, Joe?"

Lena yelled to the men from the kitchen. "Now you fellas stop talking about that. Hazel gets upset when you talk about how you kill those animals."

JC leaned closer to Joe and grinned. "Maybe, but she sure eats her share of beef when we've got it."

Lena showed them where to sit, and their two boys shot through the door in a rush with Dusty right behind them. They sat with the adults and Dusty stayed close. "Can he eat with us, Pa?"

"The table's no place for a dog. Joe?"

Joe looked at Dusty. He pointed to a place in the living room. "Sit over there, boy. Go on now." Dusty trotted into the next room and sat down, apparently content to just stare at them.

"That is one well behaved animal." Lena liked Dusty. "Better behaved than the boys sometimes." She laughed, but the boys didn't look amused.

JC was a talker and rarely let a conversation die out. "I heard about the Pepsi truck, Joe. Tough break. I bet that was a good job."

"Yeah, well you can't plan on a tractor being in the middle of the road."

"Round here you can. Still, tough break."

"I think kids will be selling soda along that road for two cents a bottle for a long time. Lots of those bottles didn't break."

"Not worth it to the company to have somebody pick 'em up. Looks like your dog ain't as well-mannered as I thought. Are you boy?" JC laughed as he roughly scratched Dusty's pointed ears.

Joe started to say something to Dusty, but JC stopped him. "He's fine right here. How's the Sinclair station going?"

Joe looked at Hazel. "Not so good. There was a reason it was closed. Not many people buying much gas right now—lots of people not working. Volumes too low. I mean, I'm glad the company let me open it up and try it, but I'm not sure we'll be able to keep it open."

Lena looked up at them while she finished chewing a bite of meat. "If you close that, what will you do? Mr. Stewart seems to want you to stay around Graham."

Hazel reached over and took Joe's hand. "We'll cross that bridge when we come to it. And we'll do it together."

* * *

Two weeks later Joe was watching his latest customer drive away, having just purchased five gallons of gas for a dollar. *Four dollars' worth of fuel today. Can't stay open if we can't sell enough.* With a sigh he locked the door and flipped the paper sign in the front door window to, 'CLOSED.' He used the Sinclair cigarette lighter the company representative had given him to light his smoke on the way to the car. He looked at it for a minute. *I shouldn't carry this around. It's made to set on a table. Funny thing—it looks like a gas pump, sort of. Huh. Hazel must have scratched off the "Sinclair" sticker on this thing. Wonder why? This might be my only souvenir from this business venture.*

At lunch, as Joe unwrapped the bologna sandwiches Hazel had brought him, he told her about the station. "I don't believe it will ever make money around here. I sold just four dollars' worth today."

She took his hands. "It'll get better, I'm sure of it." She turned to look at Dusty, who was obviously expecting part of those sandwiches. "You think so too, don't you boy."

"Hoping won't get it done, Darling. You ever hear the expression, 'Wish in one hand and...'" he paused. "'Spit in the other and see which one fills up first?'"

"I'm not sure that's how that saying goes, Joe."

"Well, it just means it's time to move on."

"How?"

"First, we've got to get your daddy to agree for us to go ahead and get married. Then we need to move to Michigan where I can get a good job in the auto factories."

"Not sure Daddy will agree to that."

"Do you want to stay here, or move up north?"

"I want to go wherever you are. If that means leavin' Graham, and Kentucky, then let's just pack up and go. My home's with you, and I don't much care where that is. Truth be told, I don't want to be the baby of a big family all my life. I want a home and a family of my own."

"Shall we talk to him tonight?"

"Guess so."

"Well, honey, I had a friend who used to say, 'If you have several frogs to swallow, swallow the big one first.'"

"That's a terrible expression, Joe. Nasty thought. Ich! And the day after Thanksgiving, too."

"Not real frogs, dear. It's just that, if you have some tough things to do, you should do the hardest one first. Get it out of the way. I think that's good advice."

"Well, Daddy will be the toughest frog in front of us. *You* gotta ask him though, not me."

"No problem, at least with the asking part. Tonight before dinner—I'll ask him then. How soon should we get married?"

"Soon as we can. You've been here two months and had two jobs. I think that's long enough, and it's sure tryin' my patience. I got my dress, and the preacher can come to the house or we can use the church. Most of the family can be there, and we can have a picnic afterwards."

"You've got it all planned, don't you?"

"I've had it planned since the first letter you sent that said you loved me."

Joe smiled. "I remember that one. The next one you sent had a red lipstick kiss on it. Well Darling, I've come all the way around the world and across this country to marry you. Let's get it done." They embraced, long and tenderly.

❋ ❋ ❋

On Friday, November 23rd, 1945, Lela was setting the table for herself, Eli, Hazel and Joe. Nobody else was expected. Several of their children and families had shared the Thanksgiving turkey— shot by Eli and cooked by Lela the day before. Today everyone was home and it was quiet at the Stewarts. Eli sat just staring ahead, not talking. Joe cleared his throat. *Now or never.*

"Something on your mind, Son?" Eli shifted his stare to Joe.

"Yes sir, there is. You probably know what I want to talk about."

"Cain't have anything to do with you not being able to keep a job, can it?"

Hazel couldn't stand for that. "Daddy, that's not fair and you know it. Joe couldn't help the accident with that farmer who didn't know how to drive, and the gas station is just fine."

Eli slowly shifted his gaze to his eleventh child. "Is it now?"

"Yes, it is, Daddy. You got no..."

"Stop Hazel. Let me tell him." Joe shifted his weight to face Eli head-on and leaned on his elbows as they rested on the table.

"Sir, the hard truth is that people aren't buying gas. They can't afford it, with so few still working and the mines letting people go. I see as many horses and mules pass the station as motor vehicles. I'm sure I take in more on the pinball machine than at the gas pumps."

"True enough, Joe. What about it?"

"We want to get married now and move to Michigan. I know I can get a good paying job at Pontiac Motors. I've tried to make it here, and it hasn't worked out so well." Hazel reached over and held his hand.

Eli again slowly shifted his gaze to Hazel. "You ready to get hitched?"

Hazel's grin was so wide her face almost disappeared behind it. "I am, Daddy. You know I am."

"Well, I reckon we probably kept you from getting married too long already, you being the age you are. You're okay Joe, and you have our blessing."

Lela stepped up close and hugged her baby girl, now far taller than she was. She didn't say a thing—she just hugged her tight.

"How soon, Joe?"

"Sir?"

"How soon you two getting married?"

Joe looked at Hazel and raised his eyebrows. She laughed and answered for them both. "Quick as we can, that's when. We can go see the preacher tomorrow and get the license on Monday. The wedding can be on Tuesday, here at the house or at the church. We could have the wedding this weekend, but with Thanksgiving just yesterday and the courthouse being closed for the weekend, that's the best we can do. Cain't get a license with them closed."

"A Tuesday wedding?"

"Why not? We've waited too long already. Everybody will be here—you'll see."

Dusty's head was in her lap. She hugged his head. "Is that gonna be okay with you, boy?" Dusty licked her hand.

THE WEDDING

Joe felt like Tuesday arrived quicker than usual that week. Even in a small-town, family-centered wedding there was apparently a lot to do to get ready. The women were cooking, the men were hunting to give the women more to cook, and Hazel's dress was getting re-stitched here and there to make it perfect.

Let's see, ten married brothers and sisters, and um, exactly twenty nieces and nephews, and the odd aunts and uncles and a few friends, why, we'll have a big crowd. I better see if that's gonna be all right. "Mama, I think there could be eighty or even a hundred people at this here wedding. Can we feed that many?"

Lela turned to look at her youngest child. "Of course we can—and one dog too, I reckon. Your sisters and sisters-in-law are all helping. JC has some beef, Phutney has venison, and all of them garden and can. Velma could feed them by herself with all the canning she does. And, Laud'a'mercy, your sister Vernie Mae is fixing a washtub sized batch of her cornbread stuffing. So we'll be just fine. The boys have already brought in over thirty squirrels and a few rabbits from the weekend hunting. Don't you worry about it child. We'll have plenty of food down at that church."

"Mama, nobody ever eats Mae's dressing—they just take it to be nice and throw it away."

"I know it. That's their business. If they hadn't started that nonsense, she wouldn't still be proud of making that nasty stuff."

She turned and fixed Li'l Hazel in her stare. "Is it kinder to hide somebody's bad cookin' and let folk laugh at them forever behind their back, or to just tell them to stop making somethin' cause nobody likes it? Anyway, go on now, child. It's all under control."

"Thanks Mama!" Hazel hugged her and ran to her next stop. She took Joe's car since he was hunting with the guys. She pulled into her sister Velma's driveway and nearly ran into the house. "Vel, you got your dress ready? And what's Henry Earl wearing?"

Velma was always cutting up and laughing. She was quite the opposite of her identical twin sister, Elma. She always wore a serious expression and didn't laugh so much as Velma. They looked identical when they dressed alike, but you could tell who was who from their expressions.

"Why Li'l Hazel, I'm just starting to give some thought to a dress for the wedding. Maybe I'll wear that old black one I keep for funerals."

"You wouldn't!"

"Of course not, silly girl. I'm all set, and Henry will have on a nice suit and tie. Since Joe don't know many folks hereabouts, Henry will stand up with him. Don't you worry none, we've got everything under control." "Well, you're supposed to, since you're my maid of honor."

"I believe that's, 'Matron of Honor,' seeing as how I'm married. It won't matter what you call me, so long as I sign that license for you and make this legal."

They both laughed.

Tuesday came and the Reverend Charles E. Daniel met them at the church. Their family and most of Graham had attended this Baptist Church forever and a day. The wedding would be inside, and the dinner would be outside.

The rehearsal was quick—just an hour before the service. Reverend Daniel lined them up. "Y'all do as I say, and pay close attention, and we won't have any problems. Don't lock your knees up or you'll pass out and keel over like a buck shot in the head, and I promise you I'll leave you there till you wake up on yore own. This lovely couple ain't going to wait on nobody or nothin' as they make their way to holy matrimony. You walk in following each other and stop right where you are. I'll do the rest. Go on, now. Be back here in an hour. And Velma, no cutting up. Henry Earl, you keep her serious now."

"Yes sir."

* * *

Lela and Eli hadn't seen all of their children in church at the same time in many years. The small Graham Baptist Church was full. Cousins, neighbors, and of course the forty members of the immediate family pushed the capacity of the small church. The children and babies were cooperating as the service started, and all was quiet as a hushed murmur covered the crowded sanctuary.

On Tuesday afternoon, November 27th, 1945, almost ten weeks after Joe was discharged from the army, the Rev. Daniel walked to the front of his church with Joe next to him and Henry Earl beside him. He indicated everyone should sit down. One of the relatives started playing the piano and Willie Curtis walked to the front. She was followed by Velma. There was a dramatic pause, after which the bride came down the aisle escorted by her daddy, Eli Stewart.

Even though it was November, it was still warm out, and the sun had been heating the church up all day. The fans were off to keep down the noise, and Rev. Daniel took out a large, white handkerchief and wiped the sweat off his speckled, bald head. He cleared his throat. "Folks, I've married a lot of Stewarts, and married off a lot of Stewarts. Eli and Lela have kept me busy these past years. But today is different. Today we are uniting a Stewart to a Michigan boy, Joe Dewey, who is a soldier, and in attendance is the extra member of their family, Dusty." People chuckled.

"Dusty saved Joe's life, and by all accounts he stays close to Li'l Hazel and protects her now. Everybody here knows that dog, and everybody who knows Joe has done met Dusty. That dog is a war hero. And while I don't usually take kindly to animals in the Lord's house, Dusty is going to sit in the back and watch the nuptials."

As if on cue, Dusty barked once. Everyone could hear the voice of young Earl Ray Cunningham from the back row as he hugged Dusty and said, "Quiet, boy. Sit still."

The rest of the service was Rev. Daniel's standard material. When he finished their vows he pronounced them husband and wife. "Joe, you may kiss your bride."

They'd grown their love from ten thousand miles apart over the course of three years, then fought to tip the scales and get Eli and Lela to allow their marriage. Joe failed at two jobs in the two months since he and Hazel had actually met, but now they were here. They were married and the next chapter of their lives—their life together—had begun. This was it! The kiss made it real!

Their embrace and kiss were epic. Rev. Daniel's church usually gave some "amens" and a few chuckles to the kiss, but this crowd started cheering, hollering and applauding like the local high school had just won the state basketball championship.

As the cheering died down, Rev. Daniel raised his voice. He had a big grin on his face. "Just sixty-five days after actually meeting each other, I present to y'all, Mr. and Mrs. W. Joe Dewey.

The couple started down the aisle toward the back.

Twelve-year-old Earl Ray gave up the struggle and let Dusty loose.

Dusty raced to Joe and Hazel, which started a new wave of cheering. With his head up and pointy ears standing tall, he trotted with them down the aisle.

> **Certificate of Person Performing Marriage Ceremony**
> TO BE DELIVERED TO PARTIES MARRIED   No. 200
>
> I, *Chas. F. Daniel*, a *minister* of the *Baptist* Church, or religious order of that name, do certify that on the *27th* day of *Nov.*, 1945 at *Graham*, Kentucky, under authority of a license issued by *Oscar Stokes*, Clerk of County Court of *Muhlenberg* County (or City), State of Kentucky, dated the *27* day of *Nov.*, 1945 I united in marriage *Wilbur J. Denley* and *Hazel Othella Stewart*, Husband and his Wife, in the presence of *Mrs. Arch Stewart* and *Mrs. Velma Cunningham*.
> Given under my hand, this *27* day of *Nov.*, 1945.
>
> *Chas. F. Daniel*, Person Performing Ceremony
> *Minister*, Title of Office
>
> Form N-12

The party started with a bang. Tubs of icy Pepsi and Dr. Pepper were in the church yard. Tables had been set up over the lawn for the meal, and women were rushing to get the food uncovered. The crowd spread out, and the bedlam seemed quieter outdoors.

Eli walked up to Rev. Daniel on the edge of the party. He nodded to his minister.

"Preacher."

"Eli."

They watched quietly from their vantage point as some of young Earl Ray's cousins carried him to one of the washtubs full of ice water and sodas and lowered him into it.

"Sorry Preacher. I hope this don't get out of hand."

"Yep. Could."

"Well, that's it then."

"Yep, I suppose so."

"She's the last of my children."

"She is."

"I don't reckon I'll be needin' your services till one of us dies."

"S'pose not. You feelin' poorly?"

"Nope. Not today." Eli turned his gentle, worn-out smile toward the preacher. "Thanks for working this out for the kids so quick." He handed the pastor an envelope.

Rev. Daniels opened it. He pulled out a dollar bill, then another one. "Well, double the others."

Eli smiled. "Last one. My baby."

The Preacher nodded as he tucked the bills in his pocket.

The party didn't end until sunset. The cleanup started the next day. The day after that Joe and Hazel packed up to leave Kentucky.

THE BIG MOVE

J oe had one small duffel with all his earthly possessions in it.

Hazel had some trunks full of clothing, a childhood ceramic doll she got just before she turned five, some odds and ends she'd picked up, and the letters Joe had sent her from Australia. The wedding gifts weren't elaborate, but they were, all in all, bulky—pots, pans, blankets and such.

"Hazel, why you packing that toy? You've had that since just before your fifth birthday. You're married, so I don't think you need a doll baby anymore."

"Mama, I'm goin' to keep this doll forever. I'll show it to my own kids someday. I am NOT leavin' it here."

"Alright, girl, do what you want. Maybe you'll have a little girl to give it to. You'll find out right quick just how much time you have for other things once you have kids."

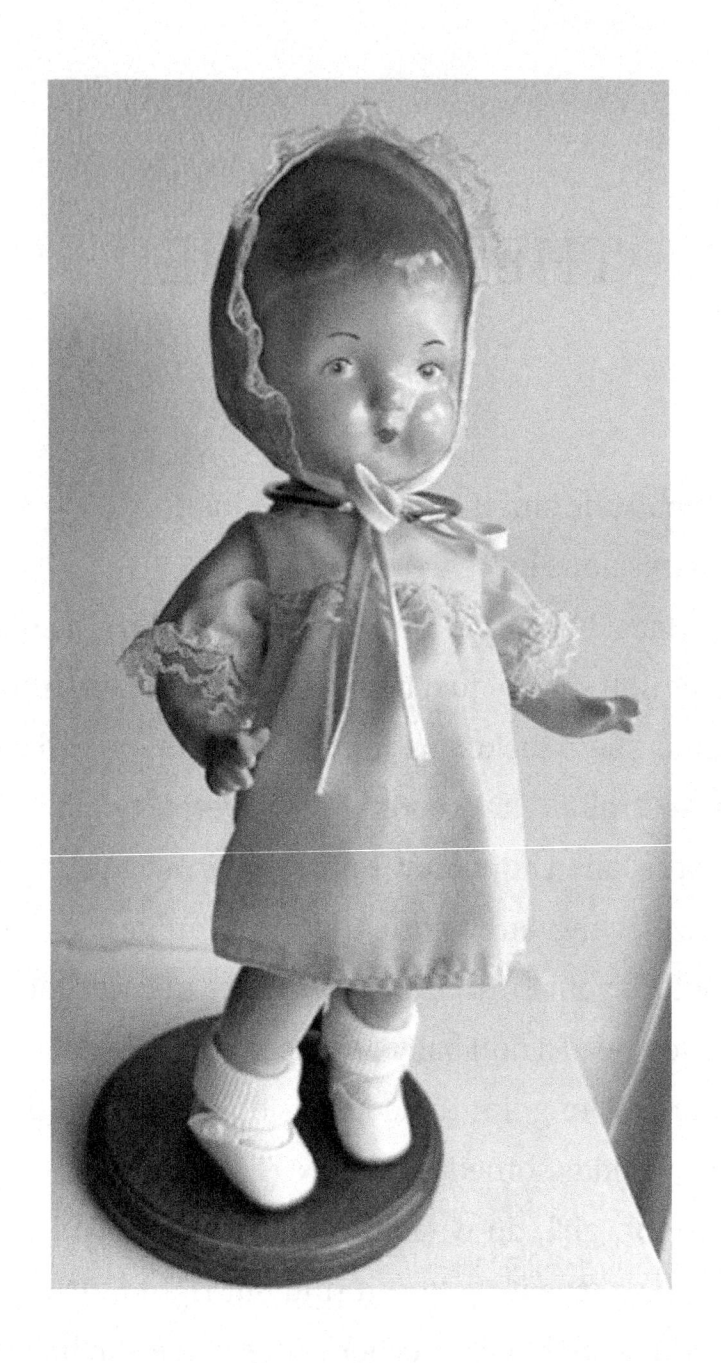

Hazel's Ceramic Doll ninety-five years later.

"Honey, this will not all go in the car. It just won't."

"Oh, Joe. Of course it will. You just go on and leave it to me and my sisters. We'll repack everything and make it fit."

Joe, Phutney and Henry Earl joined Eli under the grape arbor and watched, with some commentary, as the women tore open every trunk and box, resorted, piled up, discarded, and then stuffed the car like a Thanksgiving Day turkey. They packed soft things under the seats. They put trunks in the trunk and boxes in the back seat. They used cardboard boxes that could be crushed together so no space was left empty. They shoved two big trunks on the roof. Then they all headed for the men.

Velma was laughing, as usual, with a solemn looking Elma by her side. "Okay, boys. Tie those trunks on the roof. We did everything else for you. There's room in the front seat for you," she pointed to Joe, "and you," she pointed to Hazel, "and you," she pointed to Dusty.

"Believe you me, you'll know each other a lot better after spending fifteen or so hours together in that little bit of space that ain't filled with stuff."

The next morning breakfast was Eli, Lela, Joe and Hazel, Big Hazel and Phutney, and Felt and Willie Curtis. Everyone else had missed enough work or had too far to drive for a morning send-off.

Lela took the young couple aside. She seemed a bit distressed. "Where you staying when you get there? Have you talked with anyone?" She looked at Hazel. "Your Aunt Noni, or maybe your Aunt Lucy and Uncle Jim? I've heard from both my sisters in Michigan and they say you can stay a few days." She paused. Joe had never heard her say so much before. "Lucy won't have much space. They've got a tiny house."

Joe shook his head. "No, Ms. Stewart. My dad has rented a place for us near Pontiac. He looked for quite a while, and when he found it he put down a deposit. I guess we've been renting it for three weeks already. We'll go straight there and unload." She reached up to hug Joe. Her frail arms held him tight. "I'll miss you, Joe. You bring my baby back to visit. Hear?"

"Yes ma'am. I promise to do that as often as I can. I'll take good care of her."

There were hugs and kisses all around, and they left.

NEW LIFE

Hiring in at Pontiac Motors was easy. The work was harder because Joe's shifts kept changing. Sometimes he worked nights and sometimes he had what felt like, "normal hours."

They stayed in their rented home on Elizabeth Lake for several years. It was more like a summer cottage, but with a fireplace that kept them warm enough during Michigan's cold winters. Less than a month after they moved in they celebrated their first Christmas together, and the coldest Christmas Hazel had ever shivered through. It was also the last Christmas they spent with Stuart and Mildred Dewey.

Their life involved frequent trips back to Kentucky, and working overtime when Joe could get it.

They kept up with Joe's family, but that was limited to the occasional call and Thanksgiving dinner fixed by Mildred. Joe and Florence had their families there for that annual event, and after Serena married, her family never missed. Thanksgiving together continued long after Stuart Dewey's death.

March of 1949 was a big time, with the arrival of their first child, Patrick. Dusty extended his role as protector to the new baby. As he became a toddler, Dusty found it a challenge.

"Dusty, I've got to go do some ironing. Keep Pat in the yard." Hazel went on in and thought nothing else of it. Faithful Dusty just sat and stared at his charge. The tiny boy would sit and do nothing for long periods, then when Dusty was lying comfortably with his head on his front legs, Pat would rush toward the road, tottering as fast as his short, stubby legs could go.

Dusty was methodical and implacable. He simply ran to his young packmate, bit into his clothing, and carried him back to the house. There he would drop him, lay down and stare at him. The process was very repetitive and gave Dusty plenty of time for reflection. *This pup is all wrong. I was never this dumb as a pup. He just keeps doing the same thing over and over.*

Joe had some reflective moments after Patrick was born too. *I still smoke and drink, and my language isn't so hot. This will be bad for children, and I'm not so sure about a lot of things. Hazel seems so sure about heaven. Where am I going to be in a hundred years?*

He put away his tools and went in the house. "Hazel, would you call the minister at Oakland Avenue for me? I'd like him to come by the house this weekend for a few minutes."

"Sure Joe. What about?"

"Just call him, okay?"

"I'll do it now."

Reverend Andrew Creswell, the founding minister of the Oakland Avenue Presbyterian Church, drove out to their home on Saturday morning and spoke with Joe for a long time. Hazel hovered nearby. "What do you think Joe? You ready?"

"Yes sir, I am. Can I pray right now, here at the house?"

"Of course. God will hear you anywhere you are. Let's kneel here at the sofa."

The two men knelt together, and Hazel knelt next to Joe and put her arm around his waist. Reverend Creswell prayed for some time, then Joe talked to God haltingly and tearfully. "God, my life was a mess. I did everything wrong as a boy, and then ran off and caused more trouble. Then you gave me Dusty to keep me safe. Then you gave me Hazel to make my life whole, and now a son. Lord, I do want to go to heaven someday, and I ask Jesus to forgive me for all those things I did wrong. Please God." He choked up and stopped.

"Amen" said the pastor.

"Amen!" said Hazel.

They were regular church attenders from that day on. Hazel had been baptized in a creek, so she pushed Joe for a while to get baptized. She finally gave up. Joe waited until his youngest son, Don, was in the ministry before he was baptized. Don baptized his own young daughter first, and then his dad. Joe was the second person he baptized, followed by a dozen more than very day.

Joe switched from cigarettes to a pipe for a while, then quit smoking altogether. He never drank again. Joe was never a big talker, but now when he spoke it was always kind and clean. His friends at work didn't know what to think of him. But Joe had his family and knew his future was secure—all was well.

* * *

Two years later the second, and last surviving child came along—Donnie. He was more compliant than Pat, but between them Dusty had his paws full. One would run for the road, and the other would run toward the lake. It was a game to them. They kept trying to outsmart Dusty, but they never did. Dusty hadn't slowed down much at roughly ten years of age and continued to retrieve the little rascals and keep them safe.

* * *

Just after Don's second birthday, in 1953, Joe received a call from Mildred—his father had died. Joe's relationship with his dad had been strained over the years but had improved a lot after Joe married. He tried to be there for

Mildred, but her stoic personality didn't seem to need much from him.

He turned back to his wife, his sons and Dusty. They were his world. For the next two months life was a bit somber but fairly normal for the young family.

DUSTY'S FAMILY

The day came when Dusty chased his last car. He caught this one, but the car kept going. Dusty lay still in the road. The boys were yelling hysterically as they burst into the house.

"Mom, Dusty's hurt!"

"A car hit Dusty! Come help him."

Hazel was an emotional woman, but in this crisis she kept calm to do what had to be done. She ran to the street, told her boys to stay back, and staggered under Dusty's weight as she pulled him from the road.

"Stay here with him, boys." She ran into the house and called Joe at work. She couldn't get him, but she begged them to find him on the assembly line and have him come home. They had a family emergency.

He wasn't notified and didn't get home until after his shift. Dusty was barely breathing and Hazel was afraid to move him. Joe drove up and saw Hazel and his two little boys sitting in the grass, Dusty between them. *Something's wrong.*

He got out and sprinted to them. All three had been crying. Dusty wasn't moving. Joe dropped to his knees in the grass and held his faithful friend. His voice choked. "What happened?"

"Oh Joe, he chased a car. It didn't stop, but the boys called me...he'd been hit. He's still alive though."

Joe sat cross legged and lifted Dusty to his lap. "It's okay boy. I'm here. You've always been here for me." Joe started sobbing. The boys had never seen him cry before. Joe played with Dusty's ears as he had for almost ten years, across thousands of miles and in the forests of four countries. He stroked his neck and knew Dusty wasn't going to recover.

Joe buried his face in Dusty's neck, and the dog had just enough strength to turn his head and lick Joe's face. *My people are all with me—my family.*

He quit breathing and went limp. "Oh Dusty!"

Hazel put her arms around him—the boys reflected the intense emotion they sensed and were both crying. "Daddy?"

"Dusty's gone, boys. You need to go inside while I bury him." He held Dusty on his lap while he let each of his young sons say goodbye and hug their protector and friend one last time. Hazel sobbed as she clung to her buddy, Dusty, and finally herded the boys inside.

Joe took a shovel from the shed and started digging near the lake, but not too close. He over dug the grave. He wiped the sweat off and kept digging. It let him vent as he struck the ground with a savage fury and drove in the point of the shovel. The shovel was a blur through the tears that streaked his face. He stopped and stared up at heaven. *God, how the hell could You let something like this happen? How? All those jeeps and cars he chased, and he gets killed after we finally have a family and a home? It's not right!*

Hazel watched from the house. When she saw him stop and just stare up at the sky she thought he was done. She still waited until he turned toward the house and waved for her to come out. She brought him a blanket. Together they carefully wrapped Dusty and gently placed him in the grave. As Joe filled it in, Hazel retrieved the boys from the house. They stood at the graveside together. Joe tossed down his shovel and put his arm around Hazel to pull her close. The boys both wanted the comfort of being held by their parents. Hazel lifted one and Joe the other. They hugged as a family—the hardened soldier, the vivacious miner's daughter, and the little boys Dusty had protected throughout their young lives. All four faces were streaked with tears. Joe took a deep breath and let it out. He looked up toward heaven.

"God, I guess you let us have Dusty as long as we needed him, and I thank you for that—with all my heart. And God, I'm sorry about what I said earlier.

"Hazel, boys, Dusty's gone, but he helped us build our family, he protected every one of us, and because of him we still have each other. We'll always be Dusty's family."

This last picture taken of Dusty was at the house on the lake when Don was two.

MORE PICTURES

These are some photographs from their correspondence days during the war and their early life. These, like their letters, give an insight into their lives and views.

Some of Joe's pictures were for Hazel only and were never seen by Eli and Lela.

Joe and Dusty did everything together.

Joe at his Sinclair station

Lela resting at the close of day.

Eli finishing one of his favorite activities.

The dreaded outhouse was just behind the coal shed. Joe's young sons had to experience it, ten years later, the same way he did.

Joe met some of the native folks in Australia, New Guinea and the Philippine Islands. He sent Hazel pictures of them.

This is the only picture of Hazel's parents and all her siblings.

Back row left to right:
Lela, Eli, Velma, Elma, Flossie, Mae, Nellie, Hazel
Front row left to right:
Phutney (James), JC, Felt, Earl, Gene

GROUP DISCUSSION GUIDE

These questions are provided to help the conversation and thought processes in a discussion group. Everyone develops opinions, likes and dislikes of various characters and their actions. As you share some of your thoughts about the characters, situations and possibilities that come to mind, the following questions are designed to assist in that process.

General

1. What other books have you read that you might compare this one to, at least in genre?

2. Do you wonder how their lives turned out? Keep in mind the author is their younger son.

Style

1. Did the author's writing style add to the book?

2. Did the letters and photographs add to your enjoyment and understanding of the people and the times?

3. Did you enjoy the effort to recreate the speaking style of the people in the story?

Empathy

1. What about the book gave you the most empathy for the characters?

2. The story was true, although some details were no longer available, so the blanks were filled in by the author. Did it seem real to you?

3. Did you find at times that you put yourself in the role(s) of any of the characters in the book? If so, which ones and in what situations?

BOOKS BY DON DEWEY

(Unless indicated all are in paper and Kindle formats on Amazon)

Historical Science Fiction
Ancient Evil
The Ancients, Book 1

Ancient Power
The Ancients, Book 2

Ancient Blood
The Ancients, Book 3

Christian
Clear Truth Series
1
Angels, Questions Answered
2
Suicide and Euthanasia, Questions Answered
3
Biblical Giving, Questions Answered

Walk Through Romans
From the outlines of Howard Sugden
Foreword by Warren Wiersbe

The God of Passion

WEDDINGS-Church, State, Traditions and Culture
What You Never Knew About Weddings

Autobiographical Tool
My Life
This is a fill-in-the-blank account of your life.
Scrap Booking without all the work.
(Paperback on Amazon)

Local Interest
The Class of 1969 Pontiac Central High
(Paperback and Kindle on Amazon)

The History of First Baptist Church of Franklin, Ohio
(Kindle on Amazon)

Made in the USA
Monee, IL
03 September 2023